FOUR SCORE AND SEVEN

BY

ANDREW FEINBERG

ISBN: 978-0-692-66399-8 (ebook)
ISBN: 978-0-692-66400-1 (paperback)
www.missinglincoln.com

To the three wonderful women in my life: Adele, Caroline, and Julia.

Chapter 1

YOU NEVER KNOW when a humdrum, casually rotten day is about to turn magical.

I had made plans to get together after school with my best friend, Josh Edelstein, but then Josh said he was going to hang out with Ethan instead. "Ethan's got this thing I need to help him with," said Josh, who usually spoke very precisely for a thirteen-year-old. "It's this kind of really important thing."

"Is it a life-or-death thing?" I said, trying to twist the knife just a bit.

"Potentially could be. Maybe. Could be life. Could be death. Or maybe in between."

Thanks for the clarification, Josh. Even a mild kiss-off from your best friend can cut pretty deep.

Josh's lame explanation reminded me of the 2016 presidential campaign, which was bombarding us daily with evasions, mock-truths, and monster lies. Trust me, you never wanted your best friend to remind you of that, especially when the venomous asshat Ronald Crockenstock, the racist, coonskin-haired founder of the pay-toilet colossus Pay As You Go was setting new records for political dishonesty.

I was getting used to Josh's minidumps. Ethan was Josh's best friend (I was second best), and, on certain days, especially minidump days, I thought about arranging an accident for him. Perhaps something that would have him be medevacked far, far away, maybe to Baden-Baden, where he could stay for a year taking the waters, desperately trying to regain the ability to chew without drooling. I mean, not really, I'm a good kid—a real proper citizen—who would never do such a thing. Besides, arranging a disfiguring, debilitating accident requiring multiple full-body transfusions was no simple matter. For something I wasn't ever going to do, though, I sure did give it a lot of thought. In the realm of friendship, it can suck to be number two.

Placing second isn't great in school politics either. I had just been reelected vice president of my class, which, to put the mortifying calamity in proper perspective, meant I lost the presidency yet again. But, hey, I was vice president of the eighth grade at Forbish Milton School, one of Manhattan's best second-tier private schools. More than once I had thought of what Franklin Roosevelt's vice president John Nance Garner said of his office. Garner, a former speaker of the house who knew something about power, said the position "wasn't worth a warm bucket of piss." On the national level, vice presidents now have more responsibility than Garner had, but in eighth grade it was still a tub-of-warm-smelly-liquid kind of job. Basically, I was a glorified gofer. Okay, scratch the word "glorified." When our grade needed poster boards, markers, glitter, and streamers for a project, I was the guy who went to State News to get them. Of course, if the class president, Chad Newsome ("Gruesome Newsome" from my dispassionate perch), were to die suddenly or merely become hopelessly incapacitated, I would get his job and then I could send another dork to State News.

It was my desire for justice and, okay, vengeance that thrust me into school politics in the first place, but I'll leave that for another time.

Messing up matters further, there remained no signs that my attempts to charm the lovely Gillian Capellas were succeeding. I longed to ask her on a date—my first—but the thought of making a formal request was terrifying. If she said no, I would feel pathetic. If she said yes, I would start obsessing about the different ways I could screw up the date. I mean, what if I threw up on her? Headline: "Young Man Scarred for Life by First Date Barfing Mishap." Would I ever recover? What if she sent an incriminating selfie to everyone at school to show what a loser I was? What if the photo went viral and young men from Calgary to Perth started saying, "Well, yes, I had an awful date on Saturday—I'm now considering the priesthood—but at least I didn't throw up on the girl like that barf boy Henry Mason of New York City." Oh no, what if my name became a verb?

My fifteen-year-old sister Olivia said I could resolve the whole "courtship" situation with a single dazzling text. But Livvie believed no problem was immune to a texting solution. Her reward for brilliant texting? More texts. Her iPhone pinged non-stop, and I wondered how she could think straight. (Solution to mystery: she usually couldn't.) Livvie thought I was a moron when it came to technology and an abject failure at managing my "brand."

"Do you even know what a trend is?" she'd ask. "Would using an emoji kill you? Kim Kardashian just introduced a whole new emoji line. Do you even *know*?"

I knew now. I admired Livvie's uncanny grasp of the new, but nonetheless felt that digital avatars, like so many zombies, were busy consuming parts of her brain.

Livvie thought my brain had taken a time machine backwards. She mocked my preference for reading books printed on actual paper. "Why do you think they invented the Kindle?" she said. "You're so nineteenth century."

She had a point. Granted, I liked playing baseball and loved the New York Mets passionately. I was a pitcher and longed to be a tall fireballer on the Mets, like Jacob deGrom and Noah Syndergaard. Such dreams aside, I didn't know another kid like me. I loved Shakespeare, American history, and reading about politics. Yeah, I'd do great on Match.com—with sixty-year-olds. I just didn't know what century I belonged in. I feared it wasn't this one.

I tried to think of all the thirteen-year-olds in the world worse off than me. Of course, there were starving kids in Africa and those poor American boys who had grown massive breasts after taking the anti-psychotic drug Risperdal. At least no one came up to me and said, "Hey, nice tits." So, yes, it was a plus that I wasn't facing adolescence as a psychotic with pendulous hooters—and with the nickname, if I was lucky, of Plaintiff—but sometimes it still sucked anyway.

So I didn't look like that. Some people said I looked like Shia LaBoeuf in *Disturbia*, which I guessed was meant as a compliment, although I thought he resembled a chipmunk. Like him, I had short dark hair. I looked uncomfortable in all my photos though, and I hated them all. I had a large pimple that moved around my face. Sometimes it was on my chin, sometimes my nose, sometimes my cheek—unless it migrated to my neck. It was as if someone was playing whack-a-mole with my face.

In a small way, I was prepared for such days. I kept a bag of bird seed in my backpack—appropriated from our two finches at home—and when I had time I'd head to Central Park to feed the pigeons, sparrows, and blue jays.

The park was crowded on this clear December day, partly because it was so warm. The temperature was fifteen degrees above normal, as it had been yesterday and would be again tomorrow. This had been happening a lot lately. I found a quiet spot by a large oak and tossed the seeds strategically. First, I threw a big batch five feet away. A pigeon flew over, then a second and then a third. Soon there were six of them bobbing their heads frantically as they attacked the seeds. Then two blue jays joined the party. Six tiny sparrows and finches approached warily but remained on the periphery. They were too scared to go for the food. So I then tossed more seeds near the small birds. With the larger birds distracted, the little ones could get a decent meal. If you threw your seeds all at once, the larger and more aggressive birds would gobble up just about everything, and the small birds, who seemed to live a life of perpetual terror, would go away hungry.

Before I developed my system, feeding the birds could be a downer. Seeing the larger birds get just about all the food, I thought it was yet another case of the rich getting richer. (The bizarrely earnest Senator Lenny Plotnik, the socialist from New Hampshire who was running for president, said we had to reduce income inequality and make America more like Denmark. I was trying to create a little Scandanavia in Central Park.) My carefully calibrated feeding system was a way of making things fair, so why didn't any of the small birds ever thank me?

"I see what you're doing," a man said from behind me in a rather high, twangy sort of voice. "You're making sure the little ones get nourishment too. That is very estimable of you."

Estimable? I had read the word, but I don't think I had ever heard it spoken before. Who talked liked that?

"Thank you," I said, turning to stare at a very tall man who looked … well, exactly like a pasty-faced version of Abraham Lincoln. He was wearing a long black frock coat and a huge, black, silly-looking stovepipe hat. This was less startling than you might think because Lincoln's image was everywhere these days, commemorating the 150th anniversary of his death and of the end of the Civil War. So of course some bozo would dress up as the former president. After all, on nice days there was almost always some green dweeb by the park dressed like the Statue of Liberty, gladly posing with tourists for a fee, so why not Abe Lincoln? For all I knew, the city was swarming with Lincoln lookalikes. Certainly you saw enough of them on TV every February around Presidents' Day. I had seen Lincoln impersonators in ads so often that encountering this "Lincoln" in the flesh initially made me think less about the Emancipation Proclamation than about buying a Toyota.

"What is your name, young man?"

"Henry." I noticed that my Abe Lincoln looked very strange. It wasn't just the hat or his pallor. He kept squinting and seemed profoundly lost, as if he had just arrived from a planet with a different atmosphere and no skyscrapers. He looked as if he didn't see a single thing that reminded him of home.

"Ah, Henry, the name of kings, the name of Shakespearean heroes."

"And what is your name?"

"Before I tell you, may I ask two questions?"

I nodded.

"Where are we?"

"In Central Park. In New York City."

"What year is it?"

"You really don't know?"

"I have no idea."

My body started to tingle. "It's 2015, the 150th anniversary of Abraham Lincoln's death."

"You celebrate his *death*?"

"No, we observe it when it is a big round number. We celebrate his birthday every year as part of Presidents' Day." And then I decided to push it a bit. "My father, who is a history professor at NYU and the editor of two books about President Lincoln, says Lincoln was the greatest American who ever lived."

He smiled, a bit sheepishly at first, and then broke into a grin. "That is very nice—and after all this time, too," he said. "That is really very nice."

"You look a lot like Lincoln," I said.

"Well, I suppose I should. I am Abraham Lincoln."

"No you're not."

"But I assure you, I am."

"Do you think I'm an idiot?"

"Not at all. You seem like a nice young man."

"But you've been dead for over a century. No one comes back

from the dead. Okay, the Bible says Lazarus and Jesus did, but neither ever came up to chat with me in Central Park. I would remember if they had."

"I find this as strange as you do. This world I see looks nothing like the one I remember."

"Fine. So is there an afterlife?"

"I don't know. The last thing I remember is going to a play at Ford's Theatre. Then, somehow, I arrived here in Central Park, all these years later. That's all I know."

"I can't help thinking of what Hamlet said about the afterlife. 'From whose bourn no traveler returns.' Yet you say you have returned."

Then he began reciting:

"But that the dread of something after death,

The undiscover'd country from whose bourn

No traveler returns, puzzles the will,

And makes us rather bear those ills we have

Than fly to others that we know not of?

Thus conscience does make cowards of us all,

And thus the native hue of resolution

Is sicklied o'er with the pale cast of thought,

And enterprises of great pith and moment

With this regard their currents turn awry,

And lose the name of action."

"That was very good. I know Abe Lincoln loved Shakespeare, but lots of people know the 'To be or not to be' soliloquy. Even I know it, so it doesn't really prove anything."

"Do you like Shakespeare?"

"I love Shakespeare, but I feel weird because most of my friends don't. Okay, let's assume for the sake of argument that you really are Abraham Lincoln. I have just a few hundred questions to ask you so everybody I mention this to doesn't think I'm a lunatic. How long have you been here?"

"I just got here. You are the first person I saw."

"Why have you come back?"

"I do not know."

"Are *you* an actor?"

"No, but I loved the theater and went as often as I could once I moved to Washington."

And then it hit me. The clothes Lincoln was wearing on the night he was shot were on permanent display in Ford's Theatre. They had bloodstains. We could do a DNA test. I could play along, and if he turned out not to be Abraham Lincoln no one outside my family would ever know. I could avoid humiliation! (That was my constant goal.) So, really, there wasn't much chance I'd become known as the most gullible thirteen-year-old on the planet. I let out a deep breath. I then told the tall man about the bloody clothes and explained DNA.

"That's great," he said. "So you don't have to tell people about me until the results of the DNA test come back. By the way, why are my bloody clothes at Ford's Theatre?"

"What was the last thought you had?"

"I went with Mary and some friends to see *Our American Cousin*, and even though it wasn't that good, I remember enjoying it immensely. It was the first play I saw after the end of the war."

"You were shot in the head that night. You died the next morning at 7:22."

"I was shot? Who shot me?"

"John Wilkes Booth."

"Booth? The actor? I saw him on stage many times. He was quite good, although not as good as his brother, Edwin. Once, during an angry speech he was giving onstage, he looked into my box and glared right at me, and I thought, 'Oh, that man Booth doesn't like me at all.'"

"That would seem to have been an understatement."

"Why did Booth kill me?"

"He was a racist. He wanted the government to collapse so the South could rise again. When you gave your reconstruction speech that week he was in the crowd and thought you intended to make blacks citizens. He said, 'That is the last speech he will ever make.' And it was. The night you were shot one of his co-conspirators tried to kill Secretary of State Seward and his son Fred. They barely survived. A third man was supposed to kill Vice President Johnson, but he decided he didn't want to become a murderer, so he ran away."

"And did the Union survive?"

"Absolutely. Oh, and right now, for the first time, we have a black president, Barack Obama."

"There is a Negro president of the United States?"

"Yes. Although we now say 'black' or 'African-American' instead of Negro."

"Oh, that is marvelous! If my old friend Frederick Douglass could only be here now, he would be shouting with joy." He slapped his thigh with his hand, shook his head, and just beamed. Some color returned to his sunken cheeks. His eyes sparkled in a joyous way I had never before seen in a person, something that was never captured in any Lincoln photos. Did that mean he was an imposter or, as I had read, that photos did not reveal the complete Lincoln?

"I'm starting to think you might be who you seem to be, although I don't for the life of me know what that means. Now I'm going to ask you some questions and tell you some more things you don't know, but I warn you about one thing."

"What?"

"I know a lot more about Abraham Lincoln than most eighth graders because my father has been quizzing me about you since I was five."

"Really. Well, forewarned is forearmed."

"Okay, first, name the members of your original cabinet."

"Seward as secretary of state—another Henry, of course—Salmon Chase as secretary of the Treasury, Gideon Welles as secretary of the Navy, Edward Bates as attorney general, Montgomery Blair as postmaster general, Simon Cameron as secretary of war—what a mistake!—and Caleb Smith as secretary of the Interior. Mind you, I am not sure all the other cabinet members would get the name Caleb Smith right, he was such a nonentity. You know what was funny about Salmon Chase?"

"His name?"

"No. Nothing. He is the only man I ever met who could never laugh. And he hated his name because he said it had an unpleasant fishy quality to it. I guess it could have been worse. His uncle was named Philander."

A pretty convincing answer, but I wasn't done yet. "Who was replaced first?"

"That would be Cameron, the war secretary. He was awful at his job, but his replacement, Edwin Stanton, was wonderful."

"Who replaced Chase at Treasury?"

"There is a good story there. I did two somewhat devious things, which really was not the way I usually did business. First, you have to understand Salmon Chase. He was highly competent but always felt that, whatever position he had achieved, life should have given him more. What a formula for misery. In his case, he desperately wanted my job. He wanted it so much that I considered it a form of mild insanity. Senator Benjamin Wade, the radical Republican who was Chase's rival in Ohio, once said, 'Chase is a good man, but his theology is unsound. He thinks there is a fourth person in the Trinity.' There is some truth there.

"So keeping him around was awkward, but I figured as long as he was capable—and he was very capable—it was good to have him in the cabinet. And it was probably safer to have him inside, where I could watch him, than outside where I could not."

Just then a large jet flew overhead and the tall man stared wildly. I knew I had a lot of explaining to do. I told him about the forms of transportation invented since 1865. You know, it's not easy to tell a long-dead person that we landed on the moon forty-six years ago and have sent spacecraft on reconnaissance missions to Mars and Pluto. He took in every word, then looked at me as if I were crazy.

"A lot has changed in 150 years. Please continue with your story."

"All right. Now Chase frequently sent me letters of resignation, which I didn't accept. But when I decided the Treasury department was in good enough shape to survive without him, I finally did accept his resignation—much to his surprise! And then I went to Senator William Pitt Fessenden of Maine, who was head of the Senate Finance Committee, and asked him to become Treasury secretary but he said it was too much work and that the job might kill him. Stanton then met with Fessenden and countered with an honest if not necessarily winning argument: if the job did kill him, well, at least he would have given his life for his country. Ha! But that didn't convince him either.

"I knew he was the right man, but my powers of persuasion were insufficient. Then, behind his back, I sent his name to the Senate as my nominee."

"But what if he had still refused?"

"You have to know your man, Henry. If I dare say it, it was something I was good at. Now imagine the scene. Senator Fessenden walks into the Senate chamber and he is congratulated by dozens of senators, and they all tell him it was an inspired choice and he will do a great job. And Fessenden really was respected and the congratulations were so sincere that it became impossible for him to say, 'Well, I am actually turning down the job because I am more worried about my health than I am about the country.'"

"And I thought you were such a nice man."

"I usually was, but sometimes you have to be crafty to get things done. I was a politician."

Wow. Everything he'd said wasn't just historically correct, but he also sounded like a man recalling actual events. Could it really be him?

"Historians aren't sure why you made Cameron secretary of war. They wondered if Leonard Swett and David Davis had promised him a cabinet position to get the votes of the Pennsylvania delegates at the convention. What really happened?"

"You know about Swett and Davis? How is that possible for one so young?"

"I have studied you at my father's knee, sir."

"Indeed. Now, to answer your question about Cameron honestly, I never knew for sure. I told my people not to box me in with promises, but Cameron told me a promise had been made. So I thought that denying him a post was a risk I simply could not take. It was a political appointment in the purest sense. I absolutely did not want to make it but felt I had to. Cameron was so bad at his job that I lost a lot of sleep over my choice. My ambition to become president led me to make a selection that hurt the country and undoubtedly cost the lives of some soldiers."

"That was very convincing, but I'm still a bit confused."

"I would be shocked if you were not confused. You think I'm not confused? I always took pride in my logical mind, and everything about this situation is totally illogical. When I was . . . alive—that's the strangest way I've ever started a sentence—some people liked me and some hated me, but people knew who I was. I was accused of many things, but not of being a fraud. So now that I'm here, my first job is to prove that I'm actually Abraham Lincoln. I obviously have to do some work on my Abe Lincoln impression. And you can see how that thought might make my mind spin. Tell me, have you ever spoken to a dead person before?"

"No, I don't think so. Although I wasn't sure about my fifth-grade home room teacher, Ms. Meadows."

He cackled and slapped his side with his hand again. "You're funny." Laughter transformed his appearance in a way I had never seen in another person, as if, almost like an addict, he had an intense physical need for laughter. I made a mental note: make the man laugh.

"Thank you. Now I have just a few things to tell you. Your secretary John Hay eventually became secretary of state for two presidents. Your son Bob became a very successful lawyer and served as secretary of war to President Garfield."

"That is great for Johnny and Bob, but are you telling me that James Garfield, that blithering nincompoop from Ohio, became president? He spoke nothing but twaddle and he never liked me. How could he get elected? Did the country go mad? Was he any good?"

"He was assassinated early in his term, sir."

"What? Do they kill all the presidents?"

"They have killed four so far."

"You told me about my son Bob. What about my son Tad?"

For the first time, I thought of lying. Lincoln's son Eddie had died at age three and his son Willie at age eleven in 1862, while Lincoln was president. Could I tell him that Tad became his third son who failed to reach his twentieth birthday?

"Bob lived into his eighties."

He shot me a look that told me he knew I was being evasive. He seemed determined to get the truth out of me. "And Tad?"

"Sir, Tad died at eighteen."

His face darkened. He turned away. Then he started to shake. "No, no, no, no! This is monstrous, to have life again only to learn that another of my wonderful boys barely got to have a life at all." He knelt down and cried.

I didn't know what to do. I felt terrible for the pain I had caused. Without thinking, I put my arm around his shoulders.

He didn't respond. He just seemed to be re-experiencing a tragedy he had endured before, and at that moment I was pretty sure—as crazy and ridiculous as it seemed—that the man I was touching was the sixteenth president of the United States, Abraham Lincoln. I didn't know if I could convince another human being of this, but I knew it to be true.

"I am so sorry for what I told you about Tad. I should have kept my mouth shut. I just figured you would find out eventually."

He nodded grimly without saying anything.

"And what became of Mary?"

"She lived another seventeen years after you were shot." I did not tell him that, after Tad's death, his son Bob put her in a mental institution for a time, and she remained estranged from Bob, her only surviving son, until shortly before her death.

I desperately wanted him to know I believed him. "When I address you, sir, would you like me to call you Mr. President?"

"No, Henry," he said, patting my hand, "I don't need such formality."

"What should I call you then?"

"Well, please don't call me 'Abe.' I always hated that. I liked being called 'Lincoln,' but that doesn't seem right because of your age. Would you mind calling me 'Linc'?"

"I didn't know anyone called you that."

"No one ever did. But why not try something different this time?"

"Fine. And I'm sorry to be such a skeptic. But when you're thirteen, you're really nervous about what people think of you. Speaking of that, of all the kids in the world, why did you pick me?"

"Well, I didn't choose you, but you may have been selected because you know history and Shakespeare. Someone must have thought you would be receptive and helpful."

"But the more receptive I am, the more potential ridicule I might endure. Can you see it from my point of view?"

"Absolutely. Can you see it from mine? I never believed in any kind of afterlife. I thought the best you could hope for was to accomplish things that might live in the minds of people after you were gone. And now, it's as if God or something is playing a grand trick on me, bringing me back after all these years. A lot of people are going to doubt me no matter what, DNA or no DNA. How am I supposed to act? What am I supposed to do? Do I tell President Obama that I've come back to finish the second term I barely got to start? Probably not."

"Well, we're both pretty freaked out by this. But you see, you were special and famous for a long time. I wasn't—until you picked me, of all people, to talk to. I like to think I'm special in some ways, but I'm not *that* special."

"Maybe you are more special than you think."

"Forgive me, but I feel I have to ask you a few more things. Can you recite some Robert Burns?"

"Of course. Do you like Burns?"

"I don't really know him."

He then affected a perfect Scottish accent:

> "'Here's freedom to him that wad read,
> Here's freedom to them that wad write!
> There's nane ever fear'd that the truth should be heard,
> But they wham the truth wad indite.'"

"You're a great mimic. I think I like it, although it's a bit Scottish gibberishy to me."

"Then my mission is to expose you to more Burns. Henry, I am feeling very thirsty, as if I haven't had a beverage in a very long time. I guess I haven't. Is there a place nearby where I might get some refreshment?"

"Yes. Quite close. Excuse me, I don't know how to ask this, but since fate or something has thrown us together, I think my father might be able to help you understand why you have come back."

And then I paused, as if I were about to ask him on a date. Breathe, Henry, breathe.

"Would you come home with me and have dinner with my family? I don't mean to be pushy and, I don't know, if you have other plans . . ."

"I have no other plans. Someone may have plans for me, but I do not know what they are."

"To say we would be honored utterly fails to do justice to those words."

"Henry, I would be honored. I want to meet the people who raised a son who knows so much American history at such a young age." And I wanted to tell him how nice it was to have a grown-up guy—in this case a 206-year-old, so he was very grown-up—focus on the history I knew and ignore those facts I might have forgotten. But I didn't know how.

"First, I need to get in touch with my parents." I took out my iPhone. Linc just stared at the multicolor display. I explained what it did. "Oh, and it's a camera, too." He looked at it as if I had said, "Press this key and it turns into a rhinoceros." He was particularly fascinated by its ability to retrieve information.

"Siri, please show President Lincoln the Gettysburg Address."

She gave us the address of a dry cleaners in Gettysburg, Pennsylvania.

"Sir, this technology still has some bugs in it." So I did a little typing. "Look, here is your speech. It is the most famous speech any American has ever made."

He ignored the compliment and just stared at the words, amazed. "Do you have to be rich to have a machine like this?"

"No. There are hundreds of millions of smart-phones in the world."

"So voters today should be the best informed in history. That could be quite wonderful."

"Well, they could be, but they are not. And tens of millions of Americans don't even bother to vote. My father has a lot to say on that subject, and I'll defer to him. Linc, there is an online encyclopedia called Wikipedia that you might want to look at. It has some good information, but its entries about politics or science are often contaminated by people with political agendas. So much so, that we are not allowed to use Wikipedia as a source for some subjects at school. Anyway, here is your entry."

Linc quickly scanned it. It obviously pleased him. Then he frowned. "Given what you said about Wikipedia, I am surprised my detractors are not better represented in the piece."

"You have virtually no detractors," I said. "You are idolized in America and throughout the world. Whatever you set out to do, you did."

"Thank you for saying it that way. Still, I don't think I have come back simply to bask in my good reviews. I do not think the world works that way. Then again, given that I have come back at all, I did not think the world worked that way either." He laughed, realizing that at least some of his assumptions were no longer valid.

"Now, sir, on a lighter note, I will look up your favorite foods. Ah, here we are. Did you really like chicken fricassee?"

"It is indeed a fine dish."

"And corn muffins?"

"Also quite good."

"I'll tell my mother to make the chicken and buy the muffins for you. There, I just texted her the information. But now I have to call my father—and I have to figure out what to say."

All joy vanished as I thought of calling Dad. Here I was, with this wonderful news—news that would mean at least as much to him as it did to me, and that might even affect the whole country—but how could I tell the truth without making him think I had lost my mind? Oh man, the way things were going, even my good news was trouble.

So, thinking like a politician, I decided vagueness would be my ally. I hit speed dial. "Dad, I am bringing a very, very, very, very, very special guest home for dinner. I hope you can make it."

"Henry, you used five 'verys' in one sentence. You've never done that before. He or she must be very important."

"I believe he is. I could have used even more 'verys.' I'm not sure the world has enough 'verys.'"

"Very, very good. I'll be there."

"Linc, I warn you. My dad is going to give you a grilling like you've never received. His quizzes are legendary. Being who you say you are may not be enough for you to get a passing grade."

"Tell me more about your father."

"He is happy I love history, although he wishes I loved it as much as he does. You can tell it makes him sad when I get a history question wrong. He is proud of what I know, but he would feel better if I knew more. I think I'm the only eighth grader at Forbish Milton who had to endure pop quizzes at home. Some kids grow up afraid of monsters that lurk in closets or under the bed. Not me. I grew up terrified of getting a pop quiz when I least expected it. My father is a monstrously tough grader. 'Jack,' my mother sometimes says, 'don't treat Henry like one of your graduate students.' But he recommends great books to me all the time and when we're all sitting in a room together and I'm reading, he'll sometimes smile at me to show how happy he is that I'm trying to follow in his footsteps. Sort of."

"Our childhoods were so different," Linc said. "My father never learned to read, and he hated that I loved books. He thought reading a sign of laziness and felt I took a book with me out into the fields so I could avoid work. I read in the field only when I was taking a break, but he didn't understand that. Sometimes my reading made him so furious that he threw my books in the fire. A few times he even struck me because of it. It's strange. Some days he said my reading meant I was lazy, but other days he said it showed I had too much ambition, that I was too big for my breeches. He took it as an insult that I did not want to grow up to be a poor, uneducated farmer like him."

"What would your father have said if he'd lived long enough to see you elected president?"

He thought a bit. "I think he would have felt that the American people had made a grievous error and that I might become the laziest president in American history."

"That's so sad, especially given that you were Abraham Lincoln."

"I wasn't Abraham Lincoln to *him*. I was, 'Boy, get your plowin' done and stop messin' round with those books.'"

We kept talking as we walked. Why was this man, known for his long and mysterious silences as well as his eloquence, so chatty with a thirteen-year-old boy? The answer must have been that he felt profoundly lost—seven score and ten years lost—and so took comfort in human companionship. I was the designated human.

As we left the park, we saw the long line of horse-drawn carriages on Central Park South. Linc smiled and looked at me. He had seen something from his era! Then, after five men in shorts and T-shirts jogged past us, Linc stepped into the street and almost got hit by an Audi doing forty. I pulled him back.

"Look, I'm the leader, okay?" I said. "I think it's safer that way."

I told him my parents were both devout Improvers. My mother, Debra, who was director of marketing for *Intersections*, a magazine that was a cross between *The New Yorker* and *The Atlantic*, always thought I could be more efficient, better organized, and neater than I was. She handed out to-do lists every week to me, Livvie, and Dad. And Dad always thought I should be reading more history, which cut down on both baseball and room rehab. It was hard to satisfy both simultaneously. If I were reading a book about neat freak Stonewall Jackson, that pleased my father, but it didn't make my room less messy.

"Linc, talking about my father just made me realize something. I think I know one reason you've come back just now."

"Why?"

"Two of the worst people on the planet are leading the field for the Republican presidential nomination. The leader, by far, is Ronald Crockenstock, who's practicing a very dangerous sort of alchemy.

He's turning lies and hate into voter support. Much of what he says is untrue, but the people who like him aren't troubled by this because, first, they know even less than he does, and, second, he says everything very forcefully. 'Oh, he's so strong,' people say. 'And we need strength right now.'

"In courting evangelical Christians, he referred to what happened to Peter, Paul, and Mary on the road to Damascus."

"I thought it was just Paul who underwent a miraculous conversion on the road to Damascus."

"Of course, you're right, but Crockenstock didn't know that. Peter, Paul, and Mary are a famous singing group."

"Indeed, all three *were* in the Bible."

"That's exactly what Crockenstock said! He said he didn't want to slight Peter and Mary when he mentioned Paul."

"And people believed such hogwash?"

"Yes—maybe. Some people think that if you're really, really strong, you don't have to worry about niceties like the truth. And it's easier to appear strong if you're not hemmed in by facts. Facts can be so annoying! The people who support him seem willing to believe anything. Like his ignorance validates their own. He even said in Iowa that he would consider selecting God as his vice president. 'He'd make a good number two,' he said. 'He's been a very helpful lieutenant throughout my fantastically, monumentally successful business career.'"

"And that didn't offend people?"

"He lives to offend people. Crockenstock used his Damascus flub to segue into his plans for the Middle East, which has been a source of death and devastation for decades." I explained terrorism and talked about 9/11. I told him how calamitous a dirty bomb could be in a crowded city. "And Crockenstock uses this fear brilliantly. He said he would round up the families of terrorists and then boil them in oil, oil he would steal from their countries and then ship home to us. He would have the grandparents watch as their children and grandchildren were boiled and their eyes popped out. Then he'd boil Granny."

"And people liked this?"

"They loved it. They saw it as a great sign of strength. To them, shuddering at the thought of boiling little children to death would be a sign of weakness or, worse yet, political correctness. And then he said he knew that most Americans had at least one parent or grandparent or sibling who pretty much drove them up a tree, so those people would really like the tough way he'd treat families of terrorists. Voters are angry, and they seem to want candidates who are even angrier than they are."

"But is a president allowed to do such things?"

"Absolutely not. But I've left out the best part. He's a racist who hates almost everyone—Mexicans, Muslims, women, blacks, other Latinos, and the list goes on. He insults people at all his rallies and the crowd goes crazy for it. He is trying to engineer a hostile—a very, very hostile—takeover of the Republican Party. And for years he's been one of the biggest birthers in the United States."

"What's a birther?"

"A birther is someone who lies about where President Obama was born. He was born in Hawaii, but Crockenstock says he was born in Africa, or Asia, or on Jupiter. Now don't be confused about the difference between a birther and a truther. Truthers believe in *other* inconceivable conspiracy theories, suppositions that are so far-out they are rejected by the standard-issue nutjobs who believe almost every conspiracy theory. Nothing a truther says is true."

"You've done some interesting things with the language since I was here last."

"Finally, Crockenstock claims we should elect him because he is a genius at doing deals. But many people who have done deals with him have vowed never to do so again. Once was more than enough. Anyway, my father thinks Crockenstock is the worst person who has ever sought the presidency."

"You're making a strong case."

"But Senator Fred Arrogandez may be a close second. Crockenstock at least has a kind of roguish charm and a sense of humor, but Senator Arrogandez is a sneering, cold fish of a man, the kind who is despised by everyone who meets him. Both he and Crockenstock deny that there is global warming—hmm, this might be another reason you've come back." I explained the problem. "But Arrogandez believes all talk of climate change is nothing but a conspiracy on the part of fanatical liberals who want to expand the size of government. Oh, and he likes to say that God's law is superior to man's."

"Technically, it is not."

"Technically, he doesn't give a rat's ass. He likes saying it and his followers love hearing it. Some of the people who like him least—and this is a very, very large group—think he wants to turn America into a theocracy."

"Oh, dear. Doesn't he understand how important it is to separate church and state?"

"He absolutely, positively doesn't understand it. He emphatically rejects it. You see, today we're trying to louse up the country in new and interesting ways. Welcome back!"

When we reached my street, Fifty-Seventh Street, I pointed out the enormous new buildings in varying states of completion. Within just a few blocks there would be four new buildings at least seventy-seven stories high. "They now call this part of my street 'Billionaires' Row,' which is strange because we're not rich and don't ever expect to be, but the rich are invading our territory. Instead of elbowing us out on street level they're acquiring huge pieces of the air above our heads. The new status symbol for city living is elevation. The ultra-rich like to live very high up so they can see the city from their living rooms but not have to worry about seeing any of its people."

I paused to guide Linc into a Starbucks, where, after some consultation, I ordered him a grande cinnamon dolce latte. I took out a five-dollar bill, showed him the portrait on it, and paid for the beverage. As Linc stared at the bill, I noticed other people staring at him. Some seemed astonished that he bore such a resemblance to our sixteenth president, but then they turned away as if they figured, hey, this is probably just some late-night TV show gag.

"In 1861 I was on the ten-dollar demand note," Linc said. "It seems I've been devalued."

"You're also on the penny, but don't take it personally," I said. Then I took out another five-dollar bill and showed him the illustration on the back. "That's the Lincoln Memorial in Washington, D.C., and that's your statue right there. There is also a Jefferson Memorial and the Washington Monument. Oh, but you know about the monument. Sort of. They ran out of money in 1854, so for many years it was just a fraction of its final height."

"You're a fine guide to 2015, Henry." He smiled, then tasted his drink. "This is very good. They should open more of these places."

I laughed.

"Do you know so much history because your father forced you or because you want to?"

"Oh, I want to, but I'm not sure I want my learning to be quite as relentless as Dad does. My mother and sister don't care that much about history. They are much more into fashion and trends and social media, which means using electronic devices to communicate your likes, dislikes, and activities to a huge assortment of people who don't know what to do with their time. It has occurred to me that we are a house divided, if you will excuse the expression."

"Well, I borrowed it from the Bible, so I don't see why you can't borrow it from me. But you don't mean to imply that your house cannot stand?"

"I guess it depends what day you see us. Tonight, I think the history buffs will have a considerable advantage because of your presence, although you never know how the night will end. The females could show up with Karl Lagerfeld, Tom Ford, or Stella McCartney, in which case we're screwed."

We kept talking, as if we'd known each other for a long time. (In a sense, I *had* known him for a long time.) As my fear of looking super-gullible to my father receded, I felt joyous again, and in a kind of delightful trance. Look what was happening to my life. Here I was, Abe Lincoln's chosen guide. Maybe my father, Mr. History, would be amazed and impressed. Perhaps he would be proud. Then again, he might ask why I had neglected to bring along Washington, Jefferson, and Teddy Roosevelt, so we could recreate Mt. Rushmore at the dinner table.

Through the fog of my mixed emotions, I could see one thing clearly. Linc was definitely here for a reason, and that had serious implications for me. Could I live up to the responsibility? I didn't yet have a date with Gillian Capellas, but this felt like my date with history.

Chapter 2

WALKING HOME WITH Abe Lincoln was not easy. Naturally, I was proud to be seen with him. But I knew he was Abe Lincoln. Or thought I did. Still, I couldn't help but notice the strange and often nasty stares we got from passersby. To them I was a thirteen-year-old creep hanging out with a psycho who thought playing nineteenth century dress-up was a hoot. "Hey, it's not Halloween," two different men yelled at us.

At Park Avenue we came upon a large Chase Bank branch. "Is this bank named for my former Treasury secretary?" Linc said.

"It was named in his honor, although he wasn't the founder and his family didn't make any money from it. Its parent company, JP Morgan Chase, is one of the largest banks in the world."

I led him to the bank's row of ATMs. I needed some cash. But I didn't think of the impact my mission would have on Linc.

As the machine spat out twenties, his eyes bugged out and he recoiled. "Henry, there is money coming out of the wall!" he said. "Are all the walls now filled with money?"

"All these machines are and every bank has them. I just took out one hundred dollars. The account I share with my parents will then be debited by that amount."

"You know, I was always interested in inventions, but I never thought of a money-spitting machine. What an interesting idea. I did get a patent on a device to help boats get over shoals."

"You're still the only president who ever got a patent."

"Henry, may I see the bills from the money-spitter?"

I showed him.

"Oh, Andrew Jackson is on the twenty-dollar bill? I once hated Andrew Jackson. When Henry Clay ran against him, I happily supported Clay. But over time I came to appreciate Jackson—even if he was a Democrat. But having machines that spew pictures of the man? Your world is very strange."

"You don't know the half of it."

We arrived at my gray marble and red brick seventeen-story apartment building. "When was this built?" Linc said.

"In 1927. It's very old."

"It looks very new."

As we entered, I said hello to Boris the doorman, but then saw one of the worst specimens of humanity—certainly the worst in our building—getting off the elevator. It was beady-eyed, Brillo-haired Natalie Maggert, the only person I knew who absolutely loathed me. My mother said Mrs. Maggert was the kind of troll who hated everybody and that I shouldn't take it personally, but I did. She acted as if the greatest risk facing a thirteen-year-old male was excessive self-esteem. She needn't have worried. Now the immediate problem was what I should say about Linc if she asked.

She asked.

"That's the mangiest excuse for an Abraham Lincoln lookalike I've ever seen," she said. "Where did you dig him up?"

That's a more perceptive question than you realize, Mrs. Maggert, you walking, talking piece of water buffalo excrement. Flustered, I mumbled something about meeting him at the shelter and taking him home so he could get a decent meal.

"Well, he looks like a zombie. Lord, the type of people you and your sister bring into this building, it's just awful."

"Hope you get hit by a Fifty-Seventh Street crosstown bus, Mrs. Maggert. They move so slowly that it might merely maim rather than kill you. I'd settle for that." No, I didn't actually say that, but I sure wanted to. She walked past us with a look of disgust.

"I am impressed that you didn't insult her, for she is a woman who would be easy to insult."

"She does test my self-control."

"My friends always told me they were amazed at my capacity for withstanding abuse without retaliating. It was just my nature, I guess. But it can be helpful in public life. Tell me, does that woman who insulted us have a husband?"

"Yes, but he is very meek and usually looks depressed."

Linc nodded. "I don't doubt it."

No one was home, so I gave Linc a brief tour. He smiled when he saw the book-filled shelves lining our library/dining room. "Oh, what a banquet of words!" he said.

"Here are all the shelves with books about you and the Civil War."

"Oh, this is just wonderful, to grow up surrounded by all these books, to eat while looking at all these books. This is what a curious child should have all around him. This is one reason you know so much."

"I think my father has read every history book on the shelves, except for some of the very newest ones. Every week, new ones seem to arrive in our apartment, like a slow-motion locust infestation. And many are about you. Did you know—wait, of course you don't know—that far more books have been written about you—about fifteen thousand—than about any other individual, with the single exception of Jesus Christ? And now *you've* risen again, so there will be a new flood of books about you."

He scanned the Lincoln books briefly. "Do you have some of the books I used to enjoy?"

I led him to the shelf with Byron, Burns, and the complete works of Shakespeare. He picked up Shakespeare, then put it down and began to recite again.

> "'O, that this too too solid flesh would melt
> Thaw and resolve itself into a dew!'

"What a strange selection from *Hamlet* for me to recite," said Linc, "when the question of just how solid my flesh is may be debated by some of your fellow citizens and all the metaphysicians in the land."

"Given the circumstances," I said, "you might have picked a different *Hamlet* quote: 'There are more things in heaven and earth, Horatio, than are dreamt of in your philosophy.'"

"Apparently there are, Henry. Apparently there are."

Just then my sister came home. "Hi, Livvie, come here. I want you to meet someone."

She dropped her backpack with a thud and tossed her dark brown hair.

"Livvie, this is Abraham Lincoln. Linc, this is my sister, Olivia."

"Oh Henry, I knew you were stuck in the nineteenth century, but this is really ridiculous," my dear sister said. "Tell the tall scuzzy man he can change out of his costume now. Or whatever. If Dad sees him like this, he'll be really weirded out. You know Lincoln is always on his mind. If he sees a Lincoln lookalike in our home—and you found a really good one—he might think he has gone crazy. Take the beard off *now*. See you at dinner."

"She seems unimpressed," Linc said.

"Actually, I'm impressed she knew you were from the nineteenth century. She tries to know as little history as possible, and it drives my father nuts. Her view is that if it happened before 2012, it doesn't count."

My sister, you should know, was undeniably pretty, in a vapid brain-dead kind of way. She looked like a less intellectual Katy Perry and attracted a slew of boyfriends who knew a lot about sports and texting and bad music but not, as far as I could tell, much else. Lummoxes on Parade, I called them.

She was also the central figure in a bevy of girls, her "squad," as she called them. (Posse is so passé, she told me.) If just four of them were out on the town, they were no longer a squad. They were a "quad." It's a little embarrassing when your older sister has to teach you how young people talk today.

My sibling's abuse notwithstanding, I led Linc into the den and introduced him to TV. I was going to just channel-surf as I talked, but then thought, hey, go easy on the guy. It's hard enough for people born in the twenty-first century to cope with 1,467 channels. What must it be like for someone who was born just nine years after the end of the eighteenth century?

"First, let's start with something you know. Here is the House of Representatives in session."

"That is taking place right now?" He walked over to the TV and put his eyes very close to it, as if that would help him understand the technology.

"Right now. And here is the Senate on the next channel."

"Again right now?" He moved back to where I was.

"Yes, sir."

I clicked the remote. "And here we have one of the many strange shows about real estate that my mother and sister like. It's called *Log Cabin Living*."

"That's more like a mansion than a log cabin," said the most famous log cabin dweller in American history. "It has wood floors. We had dirt floors back in Kentucky and Indiana."

"It doesn't make you homesick?"

"It doesn't look anything like where I grew up. It looks more like the White House than one of our cabins. These moving pictures are fascinating, but I am still more interested in that thing you call the Internet. My first reaction is that it could be a tremendous force for political good, for educating voters and helping unite the nation."

"Well, it has that potential, certainly, but unfortunately the Internet gives you instant access to information that is true and information that is spectacularly false. Parts of the Internet cater solely to conservative Republicans, while other portions attract only liberal Democrats. Many sites cater to racists and people who love to hate. They often contend that President Obama is the Antichrist and that his presidency may be a sign that the apocalypse has begun."

"Oh my." He shook his head. "It sounds like newspapers back in my day, if a bit more extreme. Papers would have set political views and would get behind certain candidates and then report the news in a way that helped their cause. Some papers would run stories about my being a tyrant—'Abraham Africanus'—and an ugly gorilla even on days when I didn't do much of anything. When Mary was in good spirits, she would sometimes ask, 'Did you do anything tyrannical today, dear?' But that's how some papers saw me, and there was nothing I could do about it. I always thought that was a terrible way to educate voters, because how much would they really know about where I stood if they read only a paper that supported Stephen Douglas or George McClellan? With all your new inventions, can't you find a better way?"

Just then Mom arrived with provisions. My mom is smart and intense. She's trim with dark straight hair, and on workdays she always has this very sleek professional look. Running is one of her hobbies, and even in work clothes she looks as if she could churn out a quick five miles easily. She speaks in short, quick bursts. Sometimes just looking at her leaves me exhausted and worried that she'll assign me some new oddball chores. If I step out of my teen lair and she sees me, I'll hear about cleaning my room and bagging old clothes for Goodwill. "Maybe this weekend we could go biking? Do some apple-picking upstate? Run a 10K?"

According to Josh, who now has this new super-deep movie trailer guy voice—which is very funny since he looks eleven—the two words that describe my mother are "lovely" and "caffeinated." To calm her, my father offers cups of herbal tea and frequent foot rubs.

One thing Livvie and I bond over is Mom's extremist take on recreation and chores. "Okay, kids," Livvie will say to me, channeling Mom, "I think this would be a great weekend to build that moat we've always been talking about."

"Can't do that now, because, after the triathlon, I have to make a sofa and a new dining table," I'll respond.

My friends often talk about how good my sister and my mom look and wonder how I deal with it. Josh enjoys calling my home the House of Babes. At first, this made me feel really weird—hey, you're talking about my mother and my sister—but then it amused me. "So how are things at The House of Babes?" he'll say. "Has your sister given it up yet to this week's Lummox? Do I still have a chance?"

"Josh, that's disgusting on so many levels. I have no idea and I don't want to know. So how's life in the Asylum?" Josh's parents, unlike mine, are certifiable, but I'll get to that later.

Josh says my mother is "creepy organized," which is creepy accurate. If my father spent much of his life dwelling in the past, my mother's relentless focus was on the future. "One of these days," Josh says, "I just know she's going to give me a to-do list."

"Mom, I want to introduce you to someone very special. Very, very special. And I've vetted him, at least by my standards. Mom, I'd like you to meet Abraham Lincoln. Linc, this is my mother, Debra."

She gave me a look—a quick inventory check—just to make sure her son wasn't on drugs. "Hello, Mr. President," she said in a clipped way that was quasi-respectful but indicated she was awaiting further information before completely committing to that form of address. She was a polite businesswoman hedging her bets. "Welcome to our home. I hope you'll enjoy the chicken fricassee."

"I expect I will, ma'am. And thank you so much for going to all this trouble on my account."

"Do you need any help in the kitchen?" I said.

"No, I'm fine. Show your friend around the twenty-first century."

"How would he know where to find it?" yelled my sister, who had emerged to get something from the kitchen.

I joined her so I could get an apple for Linc. He was a notorious fruit fiend. I handed it to him and he smiled.

Just as I was about to show Linc some of my favorite history books, we heard the great historian's key in the lock. And, ever so slightly, I started to shake. "Wait, wait here," I told Linc. "I have to prepare my father. You need to hide."

I put him and his apple in the den bathroom and closed the door.

Then I went to see Dad. Dad looks like a professor. He wears tweedy jackets and slacks—never a suit—and he used to wear bow ties until Mom said he had to choose between the bow ties and her. (Like Livvie, she has very definite views on fashion.) Dad doesn't smoke a pipe but he might as well, because he looks so much like a pipe smoker. He can look both thoughtful and scattered at the same time. But when he gets focused on something, you can see how smart he really is. If you've done something wrong, you don't want him to turn that focus on you.

"Hi, Dad," I said, giving him a hug. "I have a surprise for you."

"A very, very, very, very, very big surprise, Henry?"

"Are you mocking your only son, the one who loves history almost as much as you do?"

"Yes, maybe just a little. What is your surprise? Is President Obama here?"

"You're close."

"President George W. Bush?"

"Getting warmer."

"President Clinton?"

"Warmer still."

My father rubbed his chin. I took a deep breath, grabbed his elbow, and led him into the den. I knocked on the bathroom door.

"You can come out now. Dad, I'd like to introduce you to the man I think is Abraham Lincoln. Linc, I'd like to introduce you to Professor Jack Mason, the man I think is my father."

"Professor Mason, hello. You have helped produce quite a young history scholar here," Linc said, indicating me.

"Thank you," my father croaked. His eyes kept darting from Linc to me and then back again, like a cartoon character registering overwhelming confusion. He didn't look like my father anymore. In fact, he reminded me of how Linc looked in Central Park when he realized he had risen from the dead. Dad was in shock.

"Dad, Dad, I've already quizzed him, and he not only gave all the right answers, but he cried when I told him how young Tad was when he died. And he explained why he felt he had to pick Cameron as war secretary. I think he's come back, Dad. And he's come back to us. And we can find out for sure by doing a DNA test on the blood on Lincoln's clothes in Ford's Theatre."

"Good thinking, Henry. Sir, would you like a drink?" he asked, indicating the liquor cabinet with his arm.

"No, I do not drink."

"Of course. President Lincoln did not drink. He never did. I knew that. Silly me. But I do drink, and I think this evening calls for a larger one than usual, whether or not you are who Henry thinks you are. Please excuse my agitation. Henry, could you bring me a large cocktail glass with some ice and bring a glass of ice water for your friend?"

When I returned, Dad filled his glass with more Scotch than I'd ever seen him take. He took a big gulp.

"Dad, I've prepared Linc for your grueling interrogation. He seems unafraid."

"Okay," Dad said, "let me start with a question that's never been answered. We understand that you didn't show the Gettysburg

Address to anyone until you gave it to Seward on the eve of the speech. Is that correct?"

"Yes."

"What did Seward say?"

Linc laughed. "Now you have to remember, Seward was a learned man who could talk for hours with little provocation. Sometimes when a crowd gathered outside the White House, I would go out on the balcony and say hello. The crowd would cheer and ask for more, but I would tell the people I had no speech to make.

"Not so Seward. The crowd would then disperse and walk over to his nearby home and he'd give them a two-hour speech! So the first thing Henry Seward said when he saw my little speech was, 'This is the soul of brevity itself. It is wonderful, but are you sure you don't want to add some things? Not that it needs it, but you will be finished and the crowd may not realize that you have concluded your remarks.' And on that point, Seward was absolutely right! Then he said, 'I, of course, see the little political trick you are playing here, referring only to the Declaration of Independence and not at all to the Constitution. Only the former says that all men are created equal. Some editorial writers are going to rake you over the coals for that one.'

"'Let them,' I said. 'You know, my dear Seward, in writing this I felt in my soul it is the Declaration of Independence that lays out the true meaning of the American experiment—without compromise. The Constitution may be the document that governs us, but it is filled with compromises and even some deeply disturbing portions. That's why we have had to amend it periodically.'

"And then we talked a bit more about what our country should be and could be—if only we could make it to the other side of this horrific civil war. The last thing he said was, 'I think your speech will help take us to the other side.'

"I was very moved. I hope history has given Seward his due, because he could have let bitterness be his lot once he saw the prize of the presidency go not to him but to me, a mere one-term congressman, whereas he had twice been governor of New York before becoming a senator. But he quickly became my most trusted adviser and an exceptional friend. At the end of a difficult day, I enjoyed talking to him more than to anyone else.

"I am sorry to give such a long-winded response. Oh my, I am starting to talk like Seward!"

"And you totally forgave him for initially hoping that he would be prime minister and actually run the government," Dad said, "while you would be a mere figurehead as president?"

Linc shrugged and extended his arms, palms up. "He thought I was just a backwoods lawyer. The same thought would have occurred to me if I were in his shoes. So I tried to show him his view was wrong, and he changed his mind. And there went that prime minister idea. You think I should have held a grudge?"

"Many people would have."

"And how would that have helped me?"

"Henry," my father said, "where did you find this gentleman?"

"I was feeding birds in the park and he spoke to me."

"I see. Would you two excuse me a moment?"

Dad quickly came back with an armful of Lincoln books from the library. Of course, he knew almost everything about Lincoln—but he didn't know what questions to ask a man who might actually *be* Abraham Lincoln. Looking at the books seemed to help. He rattled off dozens of questions, ranging from military strategy to political infighting to family matters to things that were deeply personal. At the outset, he sounded like Jack McCoy, the *Law and Order* prosecutor, but he gradually softened as Linc gave answers that were detailed, well reasoned, and often funny.

Then my father asked, "Were you sometimes embarrassed by your ambition?"

Linc started walking around the family room. "That's an interesting way to put it," he said. "In my twenties I thought about becoming a great man, and I saw the possibility of achieving my ambition through politics. But my reading of history and Shakespeare showed me that wanting to be great could have abominable consequences. The urge to do something memorable was as likely to result in harm as in good. I think that's why *Macbeth* is my favorite play. It is all about the horrors of ambition. It is also about the power of a wife to help drive a husband to rash and terrible deeds.

"Living with my Mary was often difficult, but she always encouraged my ambition, and not like Lady Macbeth. When I told her I wanted to be president, she said, 'You should be. I don't know anyone in the country who deserves it more and who would be more conscientious and wise if he got the job.' That is quite a thing for a wife to say. She wanted me to get the job because it would satisfy me, but I could tell that she also had a strong—a very strong—desire to be First Lady. Poor woman, she took several steps down into the gutter by marrying me. In some ways I felt I owed her a life in the White House to compensate for those grim early years."

"What was it like when Tad came in and disrupted cabinet meetings?"

Linc smiled and laughed. "First, it was wonderful. As you probably know, laughter helped sustain me when things were dark, and things were dark for most of my presidency. Tad made me laugh. I almost always felt I had at least five minutes to give him, no matter what else was going on. Even the biggest family men in my cabinet had trouble understanding this. Chase was the worst, of course. He'd just glower at me when I was playing with Tad, as if I were a simpleton or a lunatic, or some cross between the two. Even Edward Bates, my attorney general who had seventeen children, didn't seem to understand. Maybe that's because when you have seventeen children the older ones are always looking after the younger ones. For much of my time in the White House, I had just two children around because Bob was away at Harvard College. So it was hard for me to ignore Tad when he wanted attention. My cabinet would no doubt have told you I spoiled him terribly."

"Those of us who praise your political genius," Dad said, "say you had an uncanny ability to know when the American people thought the time was right to do a certain thing. The writer Gore Vidal said it wonderfully in a sentence about you: 'He had the gift of formulating, most memorably, ideas whose time had, precisely, on the hour, as it were, come.' I am thinking particularly of the Emancipation Proclamation."

"Once I got my balance as president, and it took a while, I realized one of my most important jobs was to educate the American people. I did this through speeches and letters to editors of major newspapers, something no other president had ever done. Just a digression, but Henry showed me the Internet in the park, and I immediately thought it could be a great tool for educating voters and strengthening our democracy. Henry suggested I stifle my enthusiasm and talk to you about the subject. Perhaps at dinner.

"But back to your question. In 1861 the Radical Republicans—members of my own party, mind you—told me often and loudly that I should promulgate an Emancipation Proclamation. At that point, I am embarrassed to admit, I still believed the solution to America's racial problem was, when the end of slavery came, to give blacks money to set up colonies in Central America. But I didn't really know blacks before I became president. My discussions with leaders like Frederick Douglass convinced me I was wrong, but in 1861 I knew that as much as most Americans hated slavery, they still didn't think very highly of black people. That meant they wouldn't want to fight a war primarily about ending slavery. Talking to hundreds of people who came into the White House each month to seek offices or favors helped me understand that if emancipation could be seen as a powerful tool that could help us win the war and end it sooner, then many of the people might support it.

"Slaves were an important part of the South's war machine, and if more of them came over to our side, that would hurt the South. And then, if the former slaves took up arms against the South, that would hurt them even more. In July 1862 I decided to issue the proclamation, but Seward convinced me to wait until we won an important battle. That came in September at Antietam, and later that month I announced the Emancipation Proclamation. On January 1, 1863, I issued it in a revised form."

My father got up and walked over to Linc. He shook Linc's hand, then clasped it with both hands. "Mr. President—forgive me if I don't call you Linc, but I can't—I am satisfied that you are who you claim to be. I don't know what this means, and I don't know that even a DNA test will make other people believe this, but that's what I believe. Oh no, I feel dizzy. I think I need to sit down."

"Dinner is served," my mother yelled.

Chapter 3

"DEBRA, LIVVIE, I'D like to semi-officially introduce you to the sixteenth president of the United States, Abraham Lincoln," my father said.

"We met," said my mother with a big smile. "Hello again, and we are so happy to have you. You are our first nineteenth-century visitor."

"No, Mom," Livvie said, "you're forgetting Henry."

"This is a momentous night for our family," Dad said. "And perhaps for the country as well. Henry figured out we can prove our guest's identity by using DNA analysis on the bloody clothes displayed at Ford's Theatre. Honey, your friend Angie knows an FBI agent, maybe she could help."

"I'll call her right after I serve the chicken."

We started eating, and Linc said he was very happy with the corn muffins and the chicken fricassee. "Linc," I said, "I wonder what President Polk's favorite food was."

"I don't know. I never dined with the man."

"Do you think he liked Mexican food?"

Linc laughed. "That's funny. Maybe that's why he created our phony war with Mexico. I thought he did it for land and treasure, but the food might have had something to do with it, too."

"Mr. President Lincoln," Livvie said, "could I take a selfie with you?"

"That's *the* question you have for President Lincoln?" I said. "Incredible."

As my mother explained the concept of a selfie, Dad said we had to remain quiet about Linc. "You can't tell any friends or relatives. No one."

Oh, damn. Telling Josh and Gillian was at the top of my to-do list. How could my rival Ethan top this? Reunite the Beatles? Restore the Holy Roman Empire? And I could only imagine what new-found respect Gillian would have for me. If only.

Oddly enough, Livvie put the situation into perspective. "Mr. Abe President, you are now the number one celebrity on the planet. The only person who could possibly top you is Jesus, and he isn't here right now. But *you* are. If we gave you a makeover, something a bit more in the downtown or Brooklyn style—a better hat and jacket, a shirt with some funk, maybe an earring and some ink and some beard rehab—there's no telling how many Twitter followers you could get. You would probably beat Katy Perry's seventy-nine million. I'd gladly do your social media. And you could do a reality show that would be even bigger than *Keeping Up with the Kardashians*."

"What is a Kardashian?" Linc asked tentatively.

What indeed? "Someone who is rich and famous for wanting to be famous and rich," I said.

Livvie took out her phone and showed Linc an episode. It is the one in which, I believe, Kim goes shopping for a brain.

After two minutes, Linc cried, "Oh, I can watch no more. I can't imagine that seeing so many Kardashians and seeing so *much* of each Kardashian can be good for the country."

"Well," said Livvie, annoyed, "Kim's husband, Kanye West, is going to run for president in 2020."

"Is he a senator or governor?" Linc asked.

"No, he's a rapper."

"A wrapper?"

Mom explained.

"Dear Lord, is everyone allowed to run for president these days?" Linc said.

"Pretty much," Dad said.

"Oh, and you should know," said Livvie, "that Kim and Kanye named their first child North. So her name is North West. Get it?"

"Alas, I do," Linc said. "Are you sure your society is worth saving? Oh, 'I am but mad north-north-west.'"

"Oh, that's from *North by Northwest*," said Livvie, "which is a really good movie."

"Livvie," I said, "it's from *Hamlet*."

"Since you're here, Mr. President, why don't we assume that, certain evidence notwithstanding, our society is worth saving," Mom said. "Jack, take a few minutes—just a *few* minutes—to catch President Lincoln up on key developments in American history since 1865. It is fair to assume that he has come back for a reason, and perhaps it's our job to help him figure out what that is. Then, dear, you can recommend some books. But please don't sneak up on him with a quiz."

"He quizzed me already," Linc said. "Henry wasn't sure I'd pass, but apparently I did."

"You're good at Lincoln trivia," I said.

"Are you saying my life was a trivial pursuit?"

We laughed, without explanation. Linc looked mildly confused.

"Mom, do you think this is appropriate dinner table conversation?" Livvie said.

"Livvie, we've already covered the Kardashians," Mom said. "Should we ask President Lincoln about his favorite movies? He's never seen one."

Mom explained movies.

"We could show him *Gone with the Wind*," Livvie said.

"Or not," I said.

"Just so you know, I already told our visitor he might have come back to make sure Crockenstock and Arrogandez never become president."

"That would be an excellent reason to return to life," Mom said.

"Children, I am now going to give President Lincoln the highlights, and only the highlights, of American history since his time," Dad said. "There are now fifty states, including Alaska, whose purchase was arranged by your friend Henry Seward, and Hawaii. The nation's population is 320 million, ten times as large as when you were elected president.

"Now, back to 1865. Reconstruction was difficult. The Radical Republicans did exactly what you hoped they wouldn't do and imposed frequent humiliations that increased Southern bitterness. But many white Southerners remained racists and found new ways to make blacks second-class citizens, like passing laws that required them to use separate facilities from whites. In 1896 the Supreme Court even ruled that such laws mandating 'separate but equal' facilities were constitutional."

And Dad, ever the professor, continued. And continued. He talked about the labor movement, women getting the vote in 1920, and the fact that in 2016 a woman—or a Jewish man or a psychopath—might be elected president.

"A black president to be followed by a woman president or a Jewish president? I have been away a very long time."

Then it was on to the rise of women in the workforce, the end of legalized segregation, and gay rights.

"Come on, Jack, pick up the pace," Mom said.

"Debra, only former presidents are allowed to interrupt me." Dad then doubled back to the Great Depression, the rise of the safety net for the nation's poor, the expansion of the federal government, and the surprisingly high cost of welfare and health benefits. "People are living so much longer," Dad said. "An American child born today can expect to live to age seventy-nine. So now we are debating how big government should be and exactly what rights particular groups should have. At the same time, unfortunately, public contempt for the political process has exploded."

"Dad, you left out the wars," I said.

"Henry, are you a former president?"

"No, but I think maybe I'd like to be." This surprised everyone at the table, me most of all. Oh, sure, I had fantasized about a career in politics, but my revulsion at how politics actually worked made it highly unlikely I'd ever realize those ambitions. These days, I figured, you had to be absolutely looney-tunes to want to be president. Of course, the fact that Abe Lincoln came up to me in the park did seem like a sign that I shouldn't abandon all political hope. And spending time with Linc, decency personified, also helped change my view. Which was weird because Linc's return had done nothing to alter politics. Not yet, anyway. "Look, Dad, I'm already vice president at Forbish Milton. Didn't you say Barack Obama started out as an ice-cream scooper at Baskin-Robbins and our guest here was a rail-splitter once upon a time? The vice presidency could be my stepping stone to power."

"Son, I think we need to have a long talk. Later."

"And Henry," Linc said, "I'll give you some political advice. But first I think I have to get some political advice of my own."

"Ahem, the wars?" Dad said with a bid of an edge in his voice. Maybe he didn't want Abe Lincoln, that paragon of paragons, being *too* cozy with his son. Talk about unfair competition. Dad then said the nation's long winning streak in combat had ended with Korea and Vietnam, while the battles in Iraq and Afghanistan had only left Americans feeling worse.

"Finally—" Dad said.

"Yay 'finally,'" said Mom.

"'Finally' is like my favorite word," said Livvie.

"Finally," Dad said, with a sour look, "voter alienation has grown. Participation in elections is much lower than in your time, and there is widespread belief that the most qualified people often choose not to run for office. Most people think politicians lie all the time in their quest for votes and financial support. I'll stop now."

"Yay," said Livvie.

"Linc, is it true that you never told a lie?" I said.

"Yes, Henry, but there were times when it took some effort. Now, I didn't go through my political life saying exactly what I wanted all the time. That would be ruinous. With certain audiences I would begin with position A and not mention I also held position B, which I knew would be obnoxious to them. If they asked about position B, I would say that was my view and explain why. But I wouldn't bring it up if they didn't."

"Today, a lot of politicians claim to agree with their audiences no matter what positions they hold," said my father.

"Then how can voters possibly make the right choice?" Linc said.

"They can't and they don't much of the time," Dad said.

"Are you going to talk about politics all night?" Livvie said.

"Livvie," Mom said, "Abraham Lincoln is our guest tonight. This doesn't happen all the time. What do you think we should talk about instead? Football?"

"Well, what about fashion?" Livvie said.

"I spent my entire adult life being mocked for my clothes," Linc said. "I think I got used to it."

"No offense meant," Livvie said, "but with your deep wrinkles, you could make a fortune endorsing Botox, which is a miracle wrinkle remover. I bet that could get you at least $50 million."

"Dear Olivia, I don't think I have traveled forward in time to get rid of my wrinkles, to recommend particular products, or to become fabulously wealthy."

"Maybe your hidden entrepreneur is coming out at last."

"Many older Americans," Dad said, "walk around thinking things were better in the distant past, and this is especially true of politics. What was your view of the state of politics when you were . . .?"

"Alive? Certainly there were unsavory aspects of politics—patronage, corruption, demagoguery—but politics was still able to attract many of the best people. I know that when I thought of doing something of lasting value, something that would, I hoped, benefit my fellow man, going into politics was only natural. I always felt that politics should be a noble pursuit in which people got together to work with others to try to do what is best for the nation."

"What century are you from?" Livvie said.

"The same one you accuse your brother of being from."

"The problem with politicians today is that they're all a bunch of slimy weasels," Livvie said. "They want to be famous and noticed just like the Kardashians, but they're dishonest about it. They tell people all they want to do is help them, while they're usually just doing the bidding of the people who finance their campaigns."

"Livvie," said my Dad, "that was well said. If only you were wrong."

"Professor Mason," said Linc, "why do you think I am here?"

Dad thought for a long time as he moved food around his plate. "You may be here to help unify the nation again and restore some faith in politics. Some of us think the Civil War is still being fought, to some extent, in our daily lives. I know that must sound distressing to you, Mr. President. It's not as if we have tremendous bloodshed today. Although we do have some. There has been an epidemic of white policemen killing unarmed black men and boys. But what we have most of all is enormous polarization. Some racial attitudes have improved only slightly since you were alive."

"It wounds me to hear that."

"It hurts me to say it. And no one blames you. Without you, we never would have had a black president today. But half of the opposition party doesn't believe this president was born in America. That is a lie that Ronald Crockenstock helped spread almost five years ago. Many Crockenstock supporters also think the president is a Muslim.

It is obvious that he was born in America and is a Christian. There is clear, documented evidence. That so many people ignore this evidence means there is still enormous racism in America, not to mention stupidity and general viciousness. And this helps explain the rise of a monstrosity like Crockenstock.

"Today we have a polarization pandemic. Many media outlets cater solely to extremists of both parties. Millions hear every day that their fellow citizens are doing something harmful to them because they have different beliefs. There is also a religious divide in our politics between the so-called religious right—perhaps 30 percent of the population—and everyone else. The religious right is a huge part of the base of the Republican Party, and candidates often take what most voters would deem fanatical positions to appeal to those voters.

"And on what might be the single most important issue—the warming of the earth caused by human activity—there is almost unanimous agreement among scientists but absolute disagreement between the two major parties."

"Henry mentioned this, but tell me more."

"Temperatures are increasing, glaciers are melting, and sea levels are rising. Our advances in industrialization and transportation are having a dangerous impact. We'll give you a lot to read on the subject."

"Thank you. Please continue."

"Well, on bad days I worry that the country could split in two in an ideological, and perhaps even a violent, way. But even on good days I think we've debauched the political system that you and the founders handed down to us. People who disagree about politics can hardly talk to one another now because they bring different 'facts' to the discussion. When you can't agree on the facts, it's usually impossible to agree on policy. Today, registered Republicans are so disgusted with politics that half of them support presidential candidates who've never held elected office."

The phone rang and Mom sprang up to get it. When she returned, she said, "That was the FBI."

She paused dramatically, not her usual style. This was a woman who tended not to pause for anything.

"And?" said my father.

"They'll send agents here first thing tomorrow to do a cheek swab of President Lincoln, then they'll fly it down to Washington to compare it to the blood sample. We'll know within two days."

"But some people, obviously, are going to know what these tests are for," Dad said. "If the test is positive, the results could leak out."

"The marketer in me," Mom said, "thinks you should create a plan now, before everyone in the world starts scrambling to get a piece of Abraham Lincoln. Everybody is going to want to grab part of the world's biggest celebrity."

"Do you want a piece of me?" Linc asked.

We all laughed. "Linc," I said, "that's an expression that now means 'Okay, do you want to have a fistfight about it?' Yes, we want a little piece of you, but we know we're going to have to share you with the world."

"Your mother is right," Dad said, "we need a plan. In the next hour, I'll put together a reading list for our guest. While he is studying, we should think of the best way to re-introduce him to the American public."

"Is it time for a selfie yet?"

"Not yet, Livvie, but that time will certainly come," Dad said.

"I just want a promise that I can take Linc to my school," I said.

"But I want to take him to *my* school," Dad said with a laugh.

"Having spent one year in school myself," Linc said, "I think it only appropriate if I spent more time in school. Maybe I can accommodate both of you."

"So it's a plan?" I said.

"It's part of a plan," said Mom. "Let's get to work on the rest of it. You kids still have to do your homework."

"But first, I think President Lincoln should get some sense of what he's up against. Let's show him video clips of some of the leading presidential candidates."

My heart sank. Yes, the clips might provide some comic relief, but I feared Linc would watch them and then flee forever.

Chapter 4

NO CANDIDATE WAS better at providing comic relief than Ronald Crockenstock, the pay-toilet mogul, although the laughter sometimes felt a bit hollow. He claimed that he understood the basic needs of the American people better than any of his opponents. And he was a genius at using social media, as Livvie repeatedly pointed out. With astounding frequency, Crockenstock's tweets, almost all of them savage attacks, became major news stories.

Naturally, we watched the Crockenstock compilation first.

"They said of my incredible multi-billion dollar empire that it couldn't be done and shouldn't be done but I went ahead and did it anyway and look at me now. Look at me now!" Through a combination of bullying and revenue-sharing, he had convinced a majority of construction sites in the United States to install his porta-potties.

Crockenstock inherited $200 million from his wheelchair mogul father and quickly lost half of it. He said he got the idea for his pay-toilet empire when honeymooning in Paris with his fifth wife, Norelka.

"Now Paris is my kind of city. It just oozes class. And they had pay toilets there. So I said if they have pay toilets, by God, we can bring back pay toilets to the good old U.S.A. Did you know that pay toilets date back to ancient Rome in 74 A.D.? They have a glorious history."

His bathrooms, both portable and stationary, were known for their heated, massaging seats, fancy wallpaper, and marble floors. "They're the nicest things people see in their entire lives. Most people never get to the Louvre, but anyone can use my bathrooms."

Of course, going to his loo would set you back fifty cents. Or more, in some cases. One of Crockenstock's most controversial innovations was installing change-making machines next to his toilets. The catch: you put in a dollar and got back eighty-five cents. "Exact change is important," he said. "And I plan to exact change on America, I can tell you that. If I can turn eighty-five cents into a dollar in my business, I can do the same with the U.S. budget. With me in the White House, we'll have a balanced budget in two months and a surplus in three."

"Can that be?" Linc said.

"No," we said in unison.

"Here's an excerpt from his stump speech," Dad said.

"Good people," Crockenstock bellowed, "I want you to know that America stinks, it stinks like a toxic waste dump. We suck at everything. The only thing we're good at is being bad at things. That is partly because we elected a Kenyan Muslim socialist president. Now I'm not saying he is either Kenyan or Muslim or a socialist, but others have said that and I am merely repeating it. It's a retweet, as it were. I am not responsible. But I am proud to belong to the party of Lincoln."

Linc looked very confused. "Have I become an insult?"

"No," I said, "it's Crockenstock who's the insult."

"Here he is three days ago attacking the Armenians," Dad said.

"What?" Linc said.

"No one attacks the Armenians," Mom said. "Well, except the Turks."

The next day he attacked the Turks.

"Well, I guess that would help him with the Armenians," Mom said.

At one rally, an unfortunate attendee yelled out, "What do you think of the S-S-S-Senegalese?"

"I think they're st-st-st-stupid," said Crockenstock, obviously basking in his ability to put down some African immigrants and all stutterers with one shot.

The logic seemed to be that if you weren't Senegalese and didn't stutter, this would make you feel better about yourself. I wasn't in either group, but that certainly didn't make me feel better about my country.

The next day he went after the Slovenians.

"The Slovenians?" Linc said.

"Watch," Dad said.

"The Slovenians are incredibly lazy and slovenly. In fact that's where the word comes from," said Crockenstock.

"Is that true?" I said.

"No," Dad said. "Two hours later he denied ever saying it. Four hours later he said most of his best friends were Slovenians and that his wife was Slovenian."

"Is that true?" I said.

"About the wife, no."

"He lied about where his wife is from?" I said. "Why?"

"Why not?" Dad said.

We then saw Crockenstock denying on twenty different occasions that he had ever said a certain thing. "In all twenty instances when that has been his defense," Dad said, "video exists showing that he did indeed say it."

Linc shook his head. He looked dumbfounded. In his day, people lied—but not like this.

"So that's his tell?" Mom said. "The denial?"

"Yes," Dad said. "When he says 'I never said that,' you know he said it."

"And when he says he did say it?" Linc said.

"He's often lying then as well, but not always. In that case, he seems to be lying half the time."

"So he's a pathological liar?" I said.

"I'm not sure that's the right word," Dad said. "With him, it's like breathing. You wouldn't call someone a pathological breather."

"There's a rumor that he's going to start asking audiences at his rallies which ethnic group they'd like to hear attacked that day," I said.

Dad suggested that the playbook would be:

*Attack the group an audience hates the most

*Deny ever saying it

*Say you love the group ("Some of my best friends are Mongolian")

*Then insult the candidate or reporter who pointed out Crockenstock's mendacity in the first place.

"So this is like three-dimensional chess?" Mom said.

"It's like three-dimensional chess when you steal someone's bishop and rook while they're not looking," Dad said.

"Some smart people wonder if he really wants the job," I said. "Does he have a clue that when it comes to the presidency, historians, journalists, and voters are the toughest graders out there?"

"I suspect he's having too much fun to notice," Dad said. "Everything he does is working. He lies. The crowd cheers. So he lies some more. He boasts. The crowd cheers. So he boasts some more. He is a crowd-sensitive machine, an attention-seeking missile."

The only thing Crockenstock couldn't abide, besides other people, was criticism. And the most foolproof technique for messing with his head was to refer to him as "the turd mogul." That, wrote one journalist, "was the surest way to get on his shit list."

Senator Fred Arrogandez had a very different upbringing from Crockenstock's. He was poor in the material sense, but his parents gave him a rich fantasy life. From the age of two they told him that God had decided he would be president someday. A two-term president. His security blanket featured the presidential seal (his parents called it the "national security" blanket), and every night his mother hummed "Hail to the Chief" until he fell asleep.

Telling a toddler he was certain to become president—a two-term president—had some interesting unintended consequences. Young Fred thought he was better than everyone else and repeatedly said so. From approximately the age of four, almost everyone who met Fred despised him. "I would rather we elected a hamster president," said one of his college roommates. A joke circulated in the Senate: "Why do people take an instant dislike to Senator Arrogandez?" Answer: "It just saves time." You would think being loathed by all who know you would be a serious political liability, but in the prevailing campaign ecosystem, where having crackpot ideas and millions of detractors were somehow signs of integrity, it was not.

What was a problem, however, was that Senator Arrogandez kept lagging behind Ronald Crockenstock in the dishonesty arms race. Privately, some of his advisers deplored what they saw as a yawning "fabrication gap." Many worried that he lacked the deep 24/7 commitment to lying that characterized the Crockenstock campaign. Their response to this character flaw was brilliant. They would focus the senator's deceitfulness primarily on two issues: climate change and the economy.

Most Republican candidates denied global warming in a casual who-gives-a-shit manner, but behind this lay a cold calculus. Their donors demanded denial. Denial improved reelection chances. In fact, many feared that if they said humans caused climate change, two ruthless subhumans named Koch would give tens of millions to a denier who would challenge them in the next Republican primary. But what about reality? "By the time anyone knows for sure I was wrong," one Republican senator once said, "I'll be dead, and the only thing that will bother me about being dead is being dead. Oh, you want to piss on my grave when I'm gone? Call my family for directions." (This helped explain why only 3 percent of Republicans in Congress acknowledged that human activity contributed to climate change, whereas more than 97 percent of climate scientists believed this.)

Senator Arrogandez was different. He didn't ignore the numbers. He just flat-out claimed that the numbers weren't the numbers. He massaged them so they said what he wanted them to say. "Most people are afraid to tell you such truths, but I am not. In this I am like Galileo. Let's hear it for Galileo!"

One day Senator Arrogandez brought a snowball into the Senate chamber and displayed it triumphantly.

"Linc," I said, "this is one of my favorite parts. Watch."

"What do the crazed alarmists who claim there is global warming have to say about this?" said the senator with the snowball. "I am holding it in my bare hands and I can tell you one thing, it isn't very warm!"

After watching this, Linc said, "I'm no expert on global warming, but the fact that it sometimes snows does not refute the scientific evidence that the earth is warming. This is akin to concluding that if we didn't have any fatalities on a certain day during the Civil War then we were running a non-violent debating society. This is ridiculous." Then he looked as if he had just sucked on a lemon. "And this man seems so odious and so horribly superior. You would think they sought out the worst people for the job and convinced them to run."

"They didn't have to," Dad said. "These idiots volunteered."

On the economy, the Arrogandez refrain was simple. The best way to help the poor and middle-class was to take money from them and give it to the rich via changes in tax policy. At the same time, the senator argued that he was violently opposed to income redistribution, which he defined as taking money from the rich and giving it to the poor and middle-class. "That is socialism," he said, "which is just one step from communism, which is just one step from slavery, which is just one step from saying 'Hello, Whore of Babylon.'"

Former senator and Treasury secretary Nora Blitzen came to prominence as the wife of the nation's first billionaire event planner,

Bart Blitzen. No one had ever imagined that you could become so rich as an event planner, but Bart Blitzen, using a gargantuan list of contacts, as well as cash payments and the exchange of favors, convinced people that he and only he could arrange one-of-a-kind events that would reverberate in the memory of honorees and guests forever. If, for example, you wanted Henry Kissinger and Bono to attend your wedding, only Bart Blitzen could arrange it. For an extra $500,000, he would guarantee that they would sing a duet of "I Still Haven't Found What I'm Looking For," which no guests would ever forget even if they tried.

Nora Blitzen had performed competently in high office, but for decades had a hellish time with the issue of document retrieval. When people blamed her for the document disappearances, she acted hurt. It was as if she had had the hiccups and someone had blamed her for that. Look, she seemed to be saying, some people get the hiccups and others have twenty thousand documents disappear. Stuff happens.

She did, however, occasionally try to explain. "I want to clarify something for you now," she once said. "A little while back, I pseudo-apologized for something vague that I may or may not have done but now I've forgotten what. You should as well. It would be despicable to attack me about an issue that I have already forgotten about, especially one that I think I already pseudo-apologized for. To try and force me to dredge up painful memories that could create enormous psychological damage just to prove an idiotic political point is the dirtiest kind of malevolent hatchet job I can imagine. Some of you have written that I don't disclose enough, but I have disclosed everything. Except for the things I haven't disclosed. I am full of disclosure."

"She is definitely full of something," Crockenstock tweeted. "I wouldn't trust her to keep an eye on my extra-large jockstrap."

In a year full of surprises, the early success of New Hampshire Senator Lenny Plotnik, a Jewish socialist, might have been the most extraordinary. Senator Plotnik was perhaps the most serious presidential candidate in history, and he relentlessly hammered rich people—the one percent—as the source of all evil in the country.

"The one percent control most of the country's wealth," he yelled, "which is bad, but what is worse is that they control the political process. Their unlimited contributions allow them to buy politicians. Instead of fancy cars and spectacular homes, the super wealthy now collect politicians. Enough is enough. I want them to go back to collecting Ferraris. Even after I raise their taxes, they will have plenty of money left, much more than anybody needs.

"My Democratic opponent loves Wall Street. She happily slurps up their money. Me, I hate Wall Street. I spit on Wall Street. Morally, I think Goldman Sachs is one step below the mafia. At least the mafia has the decency not to claim it is doing God's work. If I become your president, we will indict Goldman Sachs on my first day in office. We will indict them for screwing the middle class."

"Is that a crime, Dad?" I said.

"No. For Goldman it's more like a hobby."

"We will break up the big banks," Plotnik bellowed. "We will remove the 'America' from Bank of America. It will then be known as 'Bank of.' That'll show 'em.

"I, too, want to make America wonderful again. But not in the way of a certain Republican, a billionaire who is profiteering on man's most basic right, perhaps his most sacred right, the right to go to the bathroom. I want to make America as great as Denmark. I want to turn New York into Copenhagen on the Hudson. I will move Wall Street to Death Valley, where it can do less harm. This will be a huge and much-needed infrastructure project. And I promise, I will never take a nickel from Goldman Sachs."

"I think that will be an easy promise for him to keep," Mom said.

"We can do this," Plotnik hollered. "We can be Denmark. When the Plotnik revolution occurs, every American will think of himself or herself as a great Dane.

"All studies show that the Danes are happier than we are. If we were more like Denmark, Americans would be happier. Nothing is rotten in Denmark."

"I don't recall Hamlet being particularly happy in Denmark," Linc said.

"If I'm elected," Plotnik screamed, "college tuition will be free for everyone. And no one will have to pay for kale. Hail kale!"

"Free kale?" I said. "Does that make any sense?"

"Young voters love that line. They eat it up."

"Dad, that was terrible. Okay, let me get this straight. No socialist has ever come close to being elected president."

"Right."

"And no Jew has ever come close to being elected president."

"Right."

"But now a Jewish socialist actually has a chance to become the next president. Is this some kind of cosmic joke?"

"Son, this is a very strange year in America. If there were ever an ideal time for President Lincoln to return, this may well be it."

Dad then showed Linc a few clips of Dr. Ben Carson, perhaps the only man in America capable of convincing people that neurosurgeons were stupid. After an incoherent discussion of foreign policy, Dr. Carson referred viewers to his website, bencarsonisanidiot.com, for more information.

"Professor, I think you're missing the obvious point here," Linc said. "After the way Republicans have treated President Obama, it is inconceivable that they would nominate a black person in 2016. They don't seem to like black people. Please don't show me more of Dr. Carson. It is a waste of time. Cows will fly before he is nominated."

"Hey, Dad, Crockenstock is from the Bronx and Plotnik is from Brooklyn, so if they opposed each other in the general election it would be kind of like a subway series."

"Except Crockenstock doesn't take the subway. I don't think he knows there is a subway. And now I will go get some reading material for President Lincoln. Children, it's homework time."

Chapter 5

YEAH, RIGHT. HOMEWORK was all I wanted to think about. How could I concentrate on algebra, French and history when HISTORY—real history, not eighth-grade history—was being made in the next room?

I tried hard to focus, I swear. In French, our teacher Jan Fletsin wanted us to read about Louis XIV and his Code Noir, which sanctioned slavery but did so more humanely than we did in the United States because it prohibited the breakup of families. Hey, Monsieur Fletsin, if you want to talk about slavery, I've got the ultimate expert down the hall. When reading about the history of ancient Rome, all I could think of was Caligula making his horse Incitatus a senator and how Linc would soon come to realize that, at the moment, there were lots of people in the U.S. Senate who resembled the backside of Incitatus.

I was miserable. Somehow an hour passed and I accomplished nothing. Feeling guilty, I got up to get a glass of water but knew that was an excuse. I wanted to see how Linc was doing. Heck, I wanted to be sure he was still here. I found him reading aloud in the dining room, behind several huge stacks of books and a smaller pile of article printouts. I remembered that his law partner William Herndon had said Lincoln's habit of reading the newspaper aloud nearly drove him insane. Linc then frowned at what he was reading, so I turned to leave.

"Having trouble concentrating on your homework?" he said.

"Like the most ever."

"I presume it is my fault."

"It is absolutely your fault. You made my day so exciting that now I can't think about anything but you. I think you should do something about it."

"Like what?"

"Oh, I don't know, something presidential. Like revealing to the world your identity and your plan for saving us from ourselves. Then I would have a good excuse to ignore my homework."

"But you convinced me that few people would believe me without the DNA evidence. I counsel patience. Meanwhile, I have to keep reading. If I do not see you again before you go to sleep, I wish you good night. And thank you for bringing me into your family."

"You're welcome. In every sense of the word. And good night to you, Linc."

I walked over to the guest bedroom, where I found Mom changing the sheets.

"How's the homework coming?"

"A bit slow tonight. I've got other things on my mind."

"Well so do I, but in a slightly different way. It occurs to me that you and your father have thought so much about Abraham Lincoln over the years that your collective mental energy just summoned him here."

"I don't think that happened, but I assume he chose our family for a reason. Oh, I have a question."

"Yes?"

"After tonight, can we call the guest room the Lincoln Bedroom?"

"Getting ready for your White House occupancy, are we?"

"No. I just thought the name would be kinda cool. You know, put up a small plaque, the way they do at places where George Washington slept."

"That could add to the resale value of the apartment, although, if he really turns out to be Abe Lincoln, I don't see how we could ever leave."

"Linc wouldn't let us."

"How long do you expect him to stay?"

"Well, I've got five years till college, so that would be a nice amount of time."

"Somehow, I don't think it will be as long as that."

In the morning, we learned just how right she was.

When Dad, Mom, and I checked on Linc, he was still fully dressed, although he had taken his jacket off. He looked ashen. "Did any of you write on my bathroom mirror?" he said. We all said we had not, then went to see the bad news. Written in what looked like smoke was: "You have 12 days."

"Oh, no," I cried. Livvie came running to join us.

Although Linc couldn't have known how much time he would have back above ground, it's hard to believe he imagined it would be *less* than twelve more days. "I will have to read even faster," he said, "and we will all have to work harder to develop a plan that will make things better for the country. I stayed awake reading throughout the night and was never tired. It seems I no longer need sleep, so that will give me more time to work."

"I don't teach today, so I'll be around to help," Dad said.

"I can try to come home early," Mom said.

"Livvie and I can skip school to help out."

"Great idea," said Livvie, who, I believe, sometimes skipped school even when she was in the classroom.

"I'll think about that over breakfast," Dad said.

"Given how little time we have," I said, "I think Livvie and I should help with research, before the inevitable media hurricane smashes into us." Dad eventually agreed. He told me to research climate change, and he had Livvie look for ideas to make young people—and perhaps even some older people—less cynical about politics and politicians.

At breakfast, Linc ate his corn muffin but hardly touched his eggs and ham. He looked a bit like a student who had just learned the history exam scheduled for next week would begin in five minutes.

"What were some of the most interesting things you read?" I asked.

"If I might," Linc said, "I should like to wait until dinner to answer. There is much I must do. Professor, could you give me some more information about climate change and the candidates who are seeking the presidency?"

"If I do that," Dad said, "you might think less of us as a nation."

"The truth will be what it will be, no matter what we might wish. And that reminds me of a story." Linc, who had been sounding pretty morose, brightened immediately at the prospect of recounting his tale. "Well, it's a bit like the boy who, when asked how many legs his calf would have if he called its tail a leg, replied, 'five,' to which the prompt response was made that calling the tail a leg would not make it a leg."

"That reminds me of a saying of the famous football coach Bill Parcells," Dad said. "'You are what your record says you are.'"

"Or, to put it another way, you can put lipstick on a pig, but it's still a pig," I said.

"I like that one," Linc said.

"I think we've about covered the waterfront on this," Mom said. "I'm going to contact some PR people I know to help analyze our Save America plan, whatever it turns out to be. Mr. President, you're not going to suggest that our only hope is to begin colonizing space?"

"If the Republicans put a climate change denier in the White House, it may be," Dad said.

The bell rang and Livvie went to the door. As she led a man and woman toward us, she said, "It's the FBI."

The man wore a dark suit, white shirt, and a solid tie the color of dark mud, while the woman wore a dark pantsuit with a white blouse. They looked as if they were allergic to color and believed smiling could cause cardiac arrest. When they saw Linc, they barely reacted. They weren't surprised, excited, or even suspicious. They just seemed mildly annoyed, as if Linc were a messy room their mothers had told them to clean.

They told Linc what they were going to do, then the woman took a Q-tip from a wrapper and swabbed inside his cheek. She then placed the Q-tip in a plastic test tube with a stopper and put that in a plastic bag.

"This will be flown down to D.C. this morning and we should have results within two days, perhaps even sooner," said the man. He seemed ridiculously matter-of-fact, as if there weren't a chance in the world he was playing a role in one of the most astonishing events in American history. I wondered: did he know something we didn't?

The agents left. "Well, that was weird," Mom said. "But I guess it's good to know the FBI has room in its budget for robots."

"I'm glad they didn't ask to stay for coffee," Dad said. "I respect FBI agents, but I didn't want to spend any time with those two. Mr. President, is there anything I can get you?"

Linc rubbed his chin. "Yes, I would like some additional articles about what you called behavioral science, methods for motivating people to do things that are good for them. And you said it might be possible to watch more videos of the presidential candidates? That would be very desirable as well."

Linc went to do more reading. Mom left the room for a few minutes, then came back with new to-do lists for me and Livvie. Dad then said Livvie should think of ways to raise money for Linc's political foundation.

"What foundation?" I said.

"President Lincoln has some ideas for helping the country that will require money," Dad said. "He could probably get $20 million for writing a short book. He'll tell us tonight how the money would be spent."

"He knows you can't take it with you?" I said.

Dad laughed. "People said a lot of things about Abe Lincoln, but no one ever called him a moneygrubber. His wife, on the other hand, spent like a drunken sailor, but that's a different story."

Well, it was time for a deep dive into climate change. "It's the only issue my friends care about at all," Livvie said, so I agreed with Linc that discussing the subject was a good way to make inroads with young people. Linc saw the issue as crucial by itself, but he also thought it could be useful.

Most thirteen-year-olds I knew had few political passions. Some seemed to care about taxes, but they usually sounded as if they were regurgitating parental views. It struck me as odd that even kids who didn't particularly like their parents still parroted their ideas on taxes. And these were the same kids who would proclaim, "My parents know nothing about anything."

My problem was different. My parents talked politics all the time and knew a lot. They usually agreed with each other, and I almost always agreed with them. Did that make me spineless? Was I a disgrace to adolescents everywhere? Josh's parents were so out to lunch that he had a kind of anti-Pavlovian response to their opinions. If they said X, he knew the answer was Y. Or Z. Even though his response was little more than a reflex, Josh felt proud that he had his own opinions distinct from those of his parents.

If Josh, then, was his own man, what did that make me?

As I started my research, I slapped my forehead. Duh. I had been so focused on my reaction to Linc and what he might do for the nation that I didn't stop to think about what he could do for my father. Some months back, Josh, who was given to making grand pronouncements, had said, "Your mother is more successful than your father."

"Well, she probably makes more money," I'd said, "but money isn't everything."

"I don't mean money. I mean status. I think your father needs to write a book soon, probably a Lincoln book."

"But there are already 15,000 Lincoln books. Wait five seconds and there will be 15,001."

"Trust me on this, your father needs to do more to be taken seriously."

"But he edited two books of essays about Lincoln."

"Not the same. The next book has to be his entirely. No co-writer. And it has to be Lincoln."

"Josh, how do you know these things?"

He'd shrugged. "It's a gift."

Whether or not my gifted friend was right, I certainly hoped Linc's visit would, among other things, help Dad's career. But enough of that. It was time to work.

What I learned on this balmy winter Tuesday was worse than I expected. The consensus of climate scientists seemed to be that even if we reduced fossil fuel emissions dramatically, and immediately, we might still be in a boatload of trouble. If the Greenland ice sheet melted completely, that would cause the sea to rise by twenty-three feet. Add the melting of the Antarctic ice sheet, and sea levels would rise an additional eleven feet. So much for beachfront property.

I was so mad and scared that I had to get away from the laptop on my desk and just walk around the room a few times. I felt like going for a walk outside. What should I wear, a bathing suit?

Given the near unanimity of scientists that we had to start acting boldly NOW, it was even more depressing to contemplate the bizarre fact that the elected officials of one of the nation's major political parties were, or pretended to be, oblivious to the threat. But there was some hope.

The strangest thing I learned was that 48 percent of Republican voters believed human activity caused global warming. And the numbers were increasing at a rate that was anything but glacial. Yet almost no national Republican candidates articulated this view. They were all courting the wingnut base and their fossil fuel industry donors who were almost all climate change deniers. Inevitably, these candidates would one day deny they had ever been deniers. I just prayed it was soon.

This 48 percent news got me very excited—hey, I'm that kind of guy—because I knew in my gut that Linc could encourage this shift. Of course, some people would say, "How does he know anything about climate change, he's been dead for 150 years?" My job was to give him a good answer.

Whoa, lunch time already. I was making a sandwich in the kitchen when my cellphone rang. I knew I shouldn't have answered, but I always answer when Josh calls.

"Hi. So you ditched school. Are you sick?"

"Kind of. It's not too bad."

"Hey, what's all that noise back there? Sounds like the bevy of babes is up to something."

Indeed, Livvie was shouting something to Dad. "Well, Livvie stayed home to work on a project, and one of her friends came over to help."

"Livvie stayed home to do homework? I smell a rat. She doesn't do such things."

"I'm not convinced either, but that's the party line. She and her friend sure sound as if they're doing homework."

"Which friend? Is it the super-hot Cheryl? She drives me nuts."

"No, not Cheryl."

"Ava? Ava is a stone fox. And your house is the natural habitat for stone foxes."

"Easy there, guy."

"So is it Ava?"

"No." My brain was so swamped with thoughts about Linc, thoughts I couldn't yet utter, that it seemed empty of everything else. "It's Abe—ee."

"AB?"

"I must have a little cold. I said Amy. A new girl."

"And is she blazing?"

"She might be—without the beard."

He laughed. "Well, whenever I meet her, please have her scrap the beard. She's not trans, is she?"

"I don't think so, although she's been through some major changes. Some amazing shit. She's from Springfield, Illinois."

"Oh, like Abe Lincoln."

"Yeah, a lot like Abe Lincoln. You would think they were related."

"Because of the beard?"

"Yeah, that—and other things."

"Can I come over and meet her?"

"Yes. I mean, good God, no! No, I'm too sick and it's a really bad time. But let's plan for you to come over soon. How does your weekend look?"

"Saturday my grandparents are visiting the Asylum, and attendance is compulsory. Sunday should be good—assuming I survive Saturday. I think my mother and grandmother have prepared an agenda for what they should fight about. It's so much more efficient that way. No unnecessary pleasantries or preambles. And my father and grandfather will get shit-faced, argue about politics, then sit on the sofa and throw stuff at the TV while they watch the games."

"No wonder you like *Game of Thrones* so much."

"Yeah, I can relate, although I don't think we've had a beheading at home in ages. We're due for one. I plan to sneak into my room to get some work done. That's the only sanctioned form of escape."

"Okay, I'll text you ideas for Sunday."

"Fine. Just make sure your sister has some hottie friends over."

"Will do. Man, you are one horny bastard. You give puberty a bad name. You realize that if you ever made a move on my sister, I'd be honor-bound to kill you?"

"That's very open-minded of you. You're not staying home from school to train for jihad, are you?"

"Not this week."

"Okay. But good luck with the seventy-two virgins anyway."

Oh, how I wanted to tell him what was really going on. Not only did I hate lying about it, but I thought that Josh, being the fount of oracular pronouncements, might have some good ideas. Well, I'd ask him as soon as the story broke—after I apologized for misleading him.

I went back to my room and my laptop. The more I read about climate change—and the potential melting of the gigantic ice sheets—the more certain I became of two things. First, being wrong on the issue was a risk we couldn't take. Second, the climate change deniers, most of them whores to the fossil fuel mafia, had said some of the stupidest things in American political history.

Senator Arrogandez arguably had the lead in ingenious climate falsehoods. "Satellite data clearly show that temperatures aren't rising at all," he said. "This is a hoax concocted by liberals whose sole goal is to enlarge the government so that it has more control over you and me."

Whenever the senator used the word "liberal," he snarled it, so you couldn't miss its true meaning: central-planning Stalinist seeking to destroy the American way.

Not only is climate change non-existent, the senator said, it is also impossible because "God's still up there." Of course, in the annals of human history, nothing bad had ever happened on His watch.

The vicious, fact-free inanity of Crockenstock and Arrogandez was the logical apotheosis of the Republican brand. After years of dismissing facts as fancy and attacking the president of the United States as being an unentitled Kenyan Muslim socialist, this is what you got: an ignorant stew of hatred and bloodlust.

Arrogandez was a fool, but he did have the virtue of constancy. Not so James Inhofe, his colleague from Oklahoma, who was chairman of the Senate Committee on Environment and Public Works. No committee would have more impact on climate change legislation, a truly terrifying prospect. It was Senator Inhofe who said of climate change, "I thought it must be true until I found out what it cost."

I wanted to bang my head on my desk and scream. So that's how magical thinking can save the nation a fortune! It's wonderful stuff. I wish I knew how to use it.

Some other politicians seemed to think their only job was to recruit other deniers to their side, by fiat if necessary. Florida Governor Rick Scott told state employees to avoid discussing climate change. In fact, he told them never to use the phrase at all. It's hard to tell a governor he is wrong if you can't mention the subject he might be wrong about. What is especially horrifying about such Orwellian lunacy is that Florida may be more exposed to rising sea levels than any other state, except perhaps Hawaii.

Around 4:00 I decided it was tea time, so I asked Dad, Livvie, and Linc if they wanted any. All were completely immersed in their work, even Livvie. Linc was surfing the web for information, an image so incongruous that I just froze and stared.

Then it was time to give Linc our research. As I handed him my typed notes, I said, "Climate change is even worse than I thought. Unless we radically alter what we're doing, our coastal cities will be underwater. You have to speak out about it."

He nodded gravely.

Mom came home at 5:30, and we decided to order Japanese. We thought the risks of even mentioning the sushi option to Linc were high, so we got him some chicken katsu, katsu being the shortened form of the Japanese word for "cutlet."

An entirely different kind of chicken arrived at 7:30, one of Mom's genius PR acquaintances, Rory Armbrister—thin, twitchy, and birdlike—who had begun his political career as a low-level operative on the Dukakis campaign, arguably the worst by a major party since World War II. Mom had told me this important information just moments before his arrival.

"Mom, isn't that a disqualifier? Besides, I thought most of those people had committed ritual suicide."

"He's become much more thoughtful since then," she said.

I would hope so. The least thoughtful move in modern political history had been the decision to put Dukakis into an Abrams tank at a General Dynamics plant. This led to the nightmare image of a presidential candidate in a ludicrous helmet looking like a demented squirrel. Seeking gravitas, the campaign instead had gotten a visual out of a Saturday morning cartoon. The upshot? Political oblivion.

We all sat the dining table. "I think the key is to establish President Lincoln's credibility and not do anything to damage his brand," Armbrister said.

Well, that was bland, but not insane. It certainly didn't sound as if he were going to recommend Linc go anywhere near a tank.

"President Lincoln," Dad said, "since this is the closest we've ever had to a cabinet meeting in this apartment, I think it only right that you preside."

"Thank you, Professor. Mr. Armbrister, I will tell you some of my ideas and also present some from the Mason family, occasionally with my alterations. You can help me distinguish between ideas that are impossible or implausible and those that might actually work. As you know, I am fascinated by the Internet's potential. Somehow, there must be a way to make it a tool for political progress.

"One way to reduce partisanship would be to pay people to read articles that present an opposing view. Many voters only read things that buttress their views. We could change this if a nonpartisan committee selected the most compelling and least hysterical discussions of an issue. And, stealing an idea from how Professor Mason has raised Henry, readers would have to take a brief quiz about the article before they would receive payment for reading it. The payment system could give us a better educated electorate, and one less likely to demonize the opposition."

We approved. "Reading the articles could allow you to enter a lottery with the potential of making even more money," I said.

"It's possible," Dad said.

"But won't paying people corrupt the political process?" Mom said.

"Sweetie, I think we could come up with an amount small enough to encourage curiosity but not large enough to prompt a career shift," Dad said. "And if a truly bipartisan commission controls the content, I don't see a real threat of corruption. Today, the greatest corruption we suffer from is bias, a problem based on the crowding out of alternative views rather than on the money per se."

Armbrister closed his small eyes and seemed deep in thought. "I'm not sure it'll fly," he finally said. "Or we could tweak it a bit. We could have each side of an issue select the articles the other side should read."

"The problem there," I said, "is that people might pick the most hyperbolic and incendiary articles, which is precisely what we don't want. I think using a nonpartisan committee as a filter is a good one."

"Next," said Linc, "it seems that certain truths can't be uttered in politics but all kinds of lies can be. There seems to be no penalty for lying. Do you know the saying, 'Oh what a tangled web we weave when first we practice to deceive'?"

"That's Sir Walter Scott," Dad said. "We do sometimes say that today."

"Very good, sir. I just wish people paid more attention to it. Mendacity in politics seems even worse than in my day, although my view may be somewhat affected by what I've seen of this Crockenstock halfwit. Tell me, is shame an emotion that humans no longer experience?"

"No, Linc, some of us still have that one," I said. I was on firm ground here.

"The Internet could inspire truth-telling. Fact-checking by newspapers and TV networks always occurs after the fact, if you will, and that diminishes its power. I would like to see politicians on TV labeled as liars—on-screen—when they are clearly fibbing. Every time Senator Arrogandez spoke, for example, you would see a liar label next to his name—until he acknowledged that global temperatures were indeed rising."

"Would the networks go along with this?" Mom said.

"If we used the label sparingly," Linc said, "and only for absolute falsehoods as determined by a nonpartisan committee, it might work. Senator Arrogandez, for example, could continue to say climate change theory was a liberal conspiracy designed to expand the role of government. The statement is stupid, embarrassing, and dangerous, but not demonstrably false. He just can't say data show there is no climate change without being labeled a Lincoln Liar, or whatever designation people decide to use. The words 'Lincoln Liar' make me a little nervous, as you can imagine, but if that's what sticks, so be it."

"This would be really great if we could enforce it," Livvie said. "It could help people become less cynical and drive some politicians who tell nothing but lies out of business."

Again, Armbrister struck his deep-thought pose. "Not sure that'll fly," he said. Before my eyes, he was starting to *look* like a chicken. Then he tried another tweak. "Instead of using the word 'liar,' could we instead refer to a 'factually challenged person'?"

"Now I'd like to propose an idea that is exactly 150 years old. In the few days of life I had after the end of the Civil War, I thought a lot about Reconstruction. I called it 'the greatest question ever presented to practical statesmanship' and I looked forward to tackling it. That was not to be.

"One of my ideas would have been to require healthy people of the North and South to devote a year of service to the country—and especially to the South. I thought this would promote both the physical and spiritual healing of the nation, and help in the South's transition to a non-slave economy. Beyond that, I believed that the peaceful melding of Yankees and Confederates immediately after our horrible war would help both sides view the other as less alien and more sympathetic. Although there is no similar calamity to recover from today, such a program might heal some painful divisions we have discussed.

"I think we should try to raise money from the hundreds of billionaires in the United States. Olivia says they are tripping over each other in a desperate attempt to buy more status and have people notice that they're really, really rich. If I wrote ten or twenty or thirty or fifty personal letters to billionaires, I think they would pay a fortune for the privilege of displaying the framed letters in their office or home. Or so some people tell me."

"That's my idea," said Livvie, glowing.

"It's a great idea," Mom said.

"That might have flight issues," said the Chicken, thoughtfully. "Maybe you should focus on people worth $475 million or more, to expand the group."

Okay, in a different universe that could conceivably be helpful. At least it was specific. Really, really specific.

"I could also autograph five-dollar bills and collections of my speeches," Linc said. "And there could be a lottery in which the winner got to meet me and take a selfish to commemorate the moment."

"It's a selfie," Livvie said. "A selfie. And that was my idea, too."

"We could have a big concert," Linc said, "at Madison Square Garden to benefit the Lincoln Foundation. Maybe we could ask some of the biggest musicians to give a small percentage of their income to the foundation for a year or two. Young people could help make Good Government the exciting new charity. And, of course, Olivia and Debra would handle social media to raise awareness and generate excitement.

"Along with the liar labels, I think it would be valuable if all candidates and office holders had the three industries that had given them the most campaign money displayed next to their names when they spoke on TV. That way, Nora Blitzen could talk about how tough she would be on Wall Street, but then you'd see that Wall Street is her biggest benefactor and you'd think, 'Perhaps she won't be so tough.'

"I think climate change is the most important issue facing the country and the world today and some of you think I could help change the thinking of some of the deniers by stating the facts in several TV appearances and other interviews. As for some of the things these deniers say, my response is that we had idiots in my day, but yours are bigger."

"Livvie and I agree," I said, "that this is the most important issue for young people, and by stressing it you may be able to create a generation that is excited by, and really involved in, politics."

"I would like to fight political polarization while children are young, before it really begins. I think we should start political reading groups for children to expose them to more than one point of view. And by all means, pay them. Henry reads about politics all the time, but most young people don't. The Lincoln Foundation would select age-appropriate material that does a good job of expressing varying views. And, perhaps, if things grew a little less partisan, we could create adult discussion groups in different neighborhoods. We would just have to be vigilant about finding good articles on both sides of an issue.

"Granted, they will sometimes be hard to find, but they always exist. You know, I disagreed with almost everything John C. Calhoun said. After all, he was the intellectual father of secession. But he said it all exceedingly well, with great force and intelligence. Reading his speeches helped me learn how to think, and I know his eloquence made me a better speaker and writer. He just never succeeded in convincing me that slavery was good for black people."

"The next idea," Linc said, "is borrowed, in part, from a new book called *Superforecasting: The Art and Science of Prediction* by Philip Tetlock, a professor at the University of Pennsylvania, and journalist Dan Gardner. It won't surprise you to hear that people's predictions about the impact of certain laws, for example, are more accurate when they believe they will be held accountable for what they say. In politics, there is virtually no accountability. People say a certain piece of legislation will destroy the country, and, when it does not, life simply goes on. To quote Professor Mason: 'I think politicians should have a forecasting batting average, just as Lucas Duda of the New York Mets has a baseball batting average. I just hope it will be better.' This average should be posted on-screen or referenced in the press whenever the politician makes a prediction.

"Interestingly, Professor Tetlock's research shows that people with diametrically opposed views make better forecasts when they are exposed to the predictions of those who disagree with them. Both sides move closer to a middle ground. They don't necessarily agree, but they no longer tend to predict that the opponent's idea will result in the end of civilization."

Eyes closed, fingers steepled, Armbrister greeted this idea with profound concentration. "I think you may have a problem here," he said. "Would you excuse me one second? Nature calls."

When he had gone, I said, "Mom, I think Armbrister is the biggest chicken I've ever seen. Since the tank disaster, is he gun-shy about all new ideas?"

"He is a very thoughtful person," Mom said.

"I noticed," said Dad. "But does the thoughtfulness ever help? He's just stomping on all our ideas."

"But thoughtfully," I said.

"Shhh, here he comes," said Livvie.

Then the Chicken claimed the floor. "The prediction average idea might work best if you directly compared the greatest baseball players to different politicians, perhaps position by position," he said calmly, and deliberately, as he went completely off the deep end.

"What position did Bill Clinton play?" I said.

"I'll get back to you on that," the Chicken said. I had the distinct feeling that if you told the Chicken you were planning to have Abraham Lincoln parachute onto a circle in the middle of Yankee Stadium, he would think carefully, then say, "Perhaps he should land in a rhombus. That's better. Definitely a rhombus."

"Once my identity is confirmed," Linc resumed, "we will contact the *New York Times* and offer them an exclusive. When the news is out, I am told we will receive many lucrative offers. Please don't say yes too often. I'm only with you for so many days. I think I should write a short book, appear on *60 Minutes* and perhaps some other shows, and do the Cooper Union speech Livvie suggested.

"Livvie said we should put out a political CD featuring songs about lying, such as 'Lies' by The Knickerbockers, 'Lies' by Hilary Duff, 'Lies' by Billy Talent, 'Lies' by the Thompson Twins, 'Lies' by James Maslow, 'Lies' by EMF, 'Lies' by Jonathan Butler—my, that's a popular song title—'Liar, Liar' by The Castaways, 'Liar' by Three Dog Night, 'Liar' by The Cranberries, 'Lie to Me' by Brook Benton, and 'Little White Lies' by One Direction.

"We would make it clear that we are referring to where politics was, rather than where it is going. The introduction should say, 'If your argument is so compelling, why do you have to lie?'"

"Maybe you could include information about which songs were favored by which politicians," said the Chicken.

"But no one is going to publicly embrace a song about lying," Dad said.

"I was hoping some candidates might slip up," the Chicken said moronically.

"Thank you all," said Linc. "We have a lot to work with. And I have one other idea that I'm not ready to discuss yet."

"We'll give you another corn muffin or an apple if you tell us," I said.

"I thought we were trying to clean up the political process rather than resort to culinary bribery. I will tell you as soon as the time seems right."

"What is it?" Livvie said.

"It's something I should either say on television or at Cooper Union, if they will have me back after all this time."

"Can you give us a hint?" Livvie said.

"No, I apologize. I am still trying to clarify my language on this subject, and talking about it now would only confuse you and, most likely, me. It's something I have to work on alone for now. But it could be quite interesting."

I was very curious—and a little hurt. Why was Linc shutting us out? Why wasn't he asking our advice? Who did he think he was, Abraham Lincoln?

The feeling passed and I smiled inside. But I was still curious.

As the headache-inducing Chicken left the apartment, I came to understand some of Ronald Crockenstock's appeal. The pay-toilet kingpin was a nasty racist liar, but at least he seemed competent at his day job. So few people did these days.

With the Chicken gone, I said, "You know, I was getting close to throwing Armbrister out the window—I wonder if he'd fly?—but I thought of Livvie. She'd say it wouldn't be good for my brand. Mom, can we just talk to someone else from now on? I know it's very Crockenstockish of me, but I'm biased against people who don't come from our planet."

Before Mom could say a word, the phone rang. Mom got up to answer it, as usual.

She came back with a very strange look on her face. "It's the White House. They want to speak to President Lincoln."

Chapter 6

W E PUT THE call on speaker as we sat down in the family room. "Hello, Mr. President and members of the Mason family, this is Lee Patchett, deputy White House chief of staff. We just got a call from the FBI. The bureau's DNA analysis confirms a perfect match. I wanted to go over some things now and arrange to meet in New York first thing tomorrow morning to discuss how to proceed."

As happy as I was that Linc's identity had been confirmed, I had the distinct feeling that President Obama's team was about to kidnap him, metaphorically speaking.

"I'm going to send you some talking points about key issues, such as the Trans-Pacific Partnership trade agreement and immigration reform. I'll send it to Professor Mason's email. Mr. President, if you could find a way to mention the talking points at all of your public appearances, we would be most grateful." Linc started looking flustered. "So let's go over one example. You should say you think the TPP represents the best way for the world to work together to promote free and fair trade."

"But I know nothing about Pacific trade," Linc almost shouted.

"When I was president my main foreign policy concern was how to keep Great Britain and France from coming to the aid of the Confederacy."

"Well, you do date yourself, don't you, sir? We have to make sure you're current and on board. We'll smooth this all out tomorrow morning."

Patchett said he'd be at our apartment at 8:00. When the call ended, Linc was really upset. "They want to trot me out like a circus monkey to praise things I know nothing about. It's ridiculous. It would undermine everything we're trying to do. Maybe this whole effort isn't worth it." He stood up and started pacing. "Please excuse me, I need to go think."

I blocked his way in the hall. "Linc, President Obama is doing what any president would do if you suddenly showed up. He wants to steal some of your mojo."

"Mojo?"

"It means 'magic.' You have great gobs of mojo, and he would like just a little of it for himself. He wants to sprinkle himself with Abe Lincoln fairy dust. And, in his defense, this president may feel more connected to you than any other president ever has. First, he's black. Second, he was a senator from Illinois. Third, he announced he was seeking the presidency from in front of the Old State Capitol in Springfield, where your political career began."

"But that call from the White House could make this a disaster. Maybe my coming back was nothing but a big mistake."

As he closed his door, I felt a door closing on my hopes for all that his visit could accomplish. Maybe my parents had something wise to say. I rejoined them in the family room.

"That call really shook him up," I said. "He sounds as if he just wants to dig a hole and climb in. So to speak."

"That call was absolutely ridiculous," Dad said. "We've got to convince Patchett that having President Lincoln discuss the trade deal or anything else he knows nothing about could do serious harm—to both the White House and the foundation."

"But does the White House really have any power over him?" Mom said.

"No, but you don't want to alienate President Obama," Dad said. "He might say something negative about President Lincoln's ideas, or not back them as much as he otherwise might."

"I think we should tell Patchett exactly what President Lincoln is willing to do," I said. "Maybe Linc could go to the White House and say some generally positive things about the president. Maybe all the living presidents could come to the White House to meet Linc. It would be a great photo op for everyone. We'll say Linc is willing to do some things, just no humiliating extras."

"But is he willing?" Mom said.

"Right now he's weirded out," I said. "Give him time and then I'll try to cheer him up. All is not lost. Not yet, anyway."

Once again, I didn't know what to do with myself when I wasn't with Linc or trying to help him. I had some time to kill but nothing compelling to keep me focused. Linc was in a bad mood. Which meant I was in a bad mood.

Then I had an idea. I knocked on his door, entered, and said, "It's time for a road trip."

"What? Where?"

"To the West Side. Trust me."

We hailed a cab. After it had moved a few blocks, we realized we had made a mistake. The driver was a mad troll whose last name had twelve consonants and no vowels. I don't believe it was pronounceable in any language. The vowel shortfall seemed to enrage him. As we went from zero to fifty, then back to zero, then to forty, back to zero and frequently changed lanes to gain an extra inch and a half, Linc's face grew increasingly green.

"Linc, would you like to get out? We can always walk or at least get in a cab driven by a sane person."

"Maybe this is a sign I should take up drinking."

"No, it's just a sign you're in New York. Our society is still struggling with the vehicular transportation concept. Our new idea is to eliminate drivers, which seems very appealing at the moment. We'll let this madman take us through the park—there is only one lane going west so the chances of mayhem are reduced—and then we'll walk. Are you ready to talk about the White House?"

"If we must."

"You have all the leverage here. Important people, including the president, just want to be seen with you. They don't really need you to praise their policies." I told him about the idea of gathering all the living former presidents—and Linc—for a reception at the White House. "You can say nice things without embarrassing yourself. You're a gifted politician, after all. And, believe me, the former presidents are going to want to talk about your life and the Civil War rather than about some stupid Pacific trade treaty."

"Is it stupid?"

"I don't know. Every time I try to read about it, I fall asleep."

"I'm just concerned that if the White House is expecting me to be a puppet, then no one is going to take my proposals—our proposals—seriously. I'm worried that I'm going to leave in ten days with my reputation in tatters. Maybe I should just go hide until my time is up again. You know, go lie on a secluded beach and protect my good name."

Well, you know where I went with this one.

> "Good name in man and woman, dear my lord,
> Is the immediate jewel of their souls:
> Who steals my purse steals trash; 'tis something, nothing;
> 'Twas mine, 'tis his, and has been slave to thousands;
> But he that filches from me my good name
> Robs me of that which not enriches him,
> And makes me poor indeed."

"You see," said Linc, "even Iago had some good ideas. So your choice of quotation means you agree with me?"

"No, I was just showing off. And, with Shakespeare, you're always a good audience. Actually, I am certain that your good name is safe forever, unless you were to do something insanely stupid, which is not in your character."

"Don't be so sure."

"Look, the worst thing you ever did was believe General McClellan's lies for too long. And anyone in your shoes would have done the same. My father believes McClellan was responsible for more unnecessary American deaths than any American who ever lived. History has not been kind to him."

"What about suspending habeas corpus?"

"Regrettable, according to some, but certainly understandable. Don't lose any sleep over it."

I shook my head, worried that I might have offended Linc. "Uh, you know what I mean. But let's look at the big picture and, please, forget that White House asswipe for a moment. What you need right now is a hot dog from Gray's Papaya. It's the best in the city."

We had arrived at our destination. I ordered a hot dog for each of us, putting sauerkraut, relish, and mustard on Linc's without asking. Hey, the man had to learn to live a little. And he enjoyed it.

After a few bites, I said, "Linc, let me put it this way:

> "There is a tide in the affairs of men,
> Which, taken at the flood, leads on to fortune;
> Omitted, all the voyage of their life
> Is bound in shallows and in miseries.
> On such a full sea are we now afloat,
> And we must take the current when it serves,
> Or lose our ventures.'"

"You're quoting Brutus, an assassin who started a civil war. Let me give you some advice, young man. When you are speaking to someone who has been assassinated, it may not be wise to quote an assassin to him."

"I'm sure that advice will serve me well. Would you prefer I say, 'If it were done when 'tis done, then 'twere well it were done quickly'?"

"Now you're quoting Macbeth, another assassin. Henry, are you toying with me?"

"Maybe a little. But, unlike you, I only know a small number of quotations. I am merely trying to be helpful. I think you still want to bind up the nation's wounds.

We started walking south. "Look, Linc, you won the war. You saved the Union. You freed the slaves. You are now in what some of our game shows would call the 'bonus round.' You're not risking any of what you've already won. You can only win more. I think you can help the country, but if somehow it doesn't work out then it doesn't work out. You have nothing to prove.

"On our road trip today, we will visit the Lincoln Center area of New York. It was almost definitely named for you, but we can't be sure because all the records were destroyed when George McClellan Jr. was mayor of New York. He was General McClellan's son, and he, like his father, hated you."

"New York made McClellan's son mayor? I always hated New York. I always found it a strange, inhospitable city. You know that in January 1861 Mayor Fernando Wood advocated that the city secede from the Union so it could continue its profitable cotton trade with the Confederacy? And then Wood went back to Congress and almost sank the Thirteenth Amendment. This is a very bizarre city. I never got many votes here."

"Well, yes, but about Lincoln Center. Everyone assumes it is named for you, so let's agree that it is." We had reached the huge complex. "The center houses the Metropolitan Opera, the New York Philharmonic, the New York City Ballet and the Juilliard School, as well as a large theater for musicals and drama. Four blocks uptown is the Lincoln Square movie theater complex. That tall apartment building over there is Two Lincoln Square. Four blocks downtown is the Lincoln restaurant. Five blocks down Broadway you'll find the Lincoln Plaza movie theaters. Go down a bit more than a mile and you'll find the Lincoln Tunnel, the busiest tunnel in the world, which takes people under the Hudson River to New Jersey."

"How? Why?"

I explained the tunnel concept and tried vainly to explain the appeal of New Jersey, then I pointed toward Lincoln Center. "If you try to help the country and nothing comes of it, they're not going to rename this place James Buchanan Center or Millard Fillmore Center.

"And if that doesn't convince you, then think of this. How did you come to be here in 2015? Option one: You were sent here by God, but it's a mean trick. He wants you to say and do stupid things so your reputation suffers. He just wants to mess with you. Nothing good is meant to come of your return to Earth, except God may have a good chuckle. This would presume that God hasn't seen enough of human frailty yet, which is hard to imagine, especially given the current political season.

"Option two: You were sent by some kind of super-powerful random force that doesn't really care what you do. You're here by accident, so you can go hang out on a beach and maybe play a little shuffleboard. You were great in the nineteenth century and you don't owe anybody anything here in the twenty-first.

"Option three: Either God or a super-powerful force has chosen you over all other humans who have ever lived to have thirteen more days on this earth. You were not selected casually. Some force believes that your words will carry more weight than if they were uttered by anyone else. And the words themselves may be wiser—and more beautifully arranged—because they came from you. You have a chance to change the world for the better again—and this time, the whole planet may need saving.

"Of course, you could decide to do nothing. The beach and shuffleboard option remains open. But wouldn't you want to try?

"And finally, if you want to take this one step further, you could imagine that God already has an idea of what you might say to the American people and the world. And if He brought you back here, He wants you to say it. Otherwise, why summon Abraham Lincoln? Why not get someone with a really dreadful reputation—perhaps Caligula—and give *him* a second chance? I'm by no means the most spiritual person around, but I am sure you are here for a reason and that your gifts for leadership and language will again help the world. If you will let them."

"How nice is that beach you were referring to?"

"Linc!"

"Just making a little joke, Henry. How did one so young get so wise? In my vanity, I sometimes thought I was one of the world's most logical men, and here you are using logic to trip me up."

"I may be wise on the subject of you, but I'm not so wise on the subject of me. If I were, I'd find a way of getting a date with Gillian Capellas."

"I don't think it would be wise to seek my advice on courtship."

I laughed. "No, you are the man who wrote a letter to Mary Owens making it clear why she shouldn't marry you."

"It was a good letter. I thought I made my case well." He laughed. "Have you tried telling this young lady a funny story?"

"Not exactly."

"In my experience, men really like funny stories. Women? Sometimes yes and sometimes no."

He paused and looked directly at me. "Henry, you know what we are?"

I gulped. "What?"

"We're friends. I think if you and I were both thirteen back in Indiana, we would have been very, very good friends."

I was not sure what part of him, if any, it was okay to touch. I thought of his shoulder and then his hand, but somehow touched his elbow. I mean, you couldn't very well bro-hug a former president who was 193 years your elder. "Thank you. Thank you very much. I think so too."

We were now standing right at the wonderful, lighted, circular granite fountain at the heart of Lincoln Center.

"Are you allowed to go in the fountain?" Linc said.

"I suspect normal people are not. But if you're the Lincoln in Lincoln Center, I think you might get a pass. Just don't get soaked."

And then, I once again watched my life unfold as if I were in a trance. Linc took off his boots and socks and rolled up his pant legs. He stepped into the fountain. Then he smiled and started to do a little dance.

All the splashing notwithstanding, this was nothing like Gene Kelly's controlled frolicking in *Singin' in the Rain*. Linc's style of movement was more like a hippopotamus fending off a family of crocodiles. But he was smiling, and given his earlier despondency, I felt some sense of accomplishment in that.

I tried hard not to laugh. "Linc, this reminds me of a story. There was a young man named Abraham Lincoln, and upon seeing Mary Todd of Kentucky at a dance, he told her he wanted to dance with her in the worst way. 'And that's precisely what he proceeded to do,' said Mary."

"Are you criticizing my dancing?"

"Not at all. Just passing along a story I read."

"And what's the moral lesson to be drawn from that?"

"The moral lesson," said the policeman who had just arrived at the side of the fountain, "is that you can't dance in the fountain at Lincoln Center even if you look just like Abe Lincoln."

Of course, we couldn't tell the officer that this was Lincoln of Lincoln Center. Although I was tempted.

"You're lucky I'm not going to give you a summons for trespassing and for strange and truly awful public dancing. But I'm feeling bighearted tonight and Lincoln is my favorite president. So, 'with charity for all' and no malice neither, I'm going to let you off with a very stern warning. You really, really should not dance in public."

We thanked the policeman for not arresting us, then Linc dried off as best he could. "After the *New York Times* piece comes out," I said, "that cop is going to have quite a story to tell."

"But will anyone believe him?" Linc said. "One of the problems with the truth is that it often seems so unlikely."

Yes, you could say that, I thought, as I watched the sixteenth president of the United States put on his socks and boots after dancing in the fountain at Lincoln Center.

Chapter 7

A T 8:00 THE next morning, Lee Patchett, the deputy White House chief of staff, rang our bell. He was a wiry, intense guy with very short brown hair. He had some of my mother's born-to-run quality, although his had a layer of anger to it. Unlike the impassive FBI agents, this guy seemed prepared for a fight. We sat at the dining table and gave him some coffee, the last thing he seemed to need.

I couldn't wait for the meeting to be over for two reasons. First, this guy could really torpedo our plans if he turned Linc into an administration mouthpiece. Second, the *New York Times* was sending two reporters and a photographer at 10:00. If Linc survived the meeting with the Obama White House, his identity was about to be revealed to the world.

Linc began by telling Patchett he would make no public comments on any issues he had not studied. So no words on the TPP. No words on Obamacare or foreign policy, especially as it applied to the Middle East. He would, however, gladly praise the president for his work on climate change and race relations.

Patchett's face turned bright red. "That won't do. You owe us more than that. We told you what we wanted. We even authenticated you! All we're asking is that you use a few talking points on several issues vitally important to President Obama."

"But don't you see," said Linc, "that would make us both look stupid. People would think President Obama's only concern with my return is that I put my imprimatur on his policies. That can't conceivably be the reason I've come back, to endorse the policies of a sitting president who can't even run again. It's so petty, people will laugh—and it won't help your cause. Sir, I can certainly promise I won't say anything bad about your boss. I like him. I just refuse to be his lap dog."

They went round and round for another half hour, with Patchett alternating between abject begging and remarkable belligerence.

"I'll gladly talk to the president directly if that would make your life easier," Linc said. "I once had his job, you know. I know something about this. Beware, though, I won't say anything I don't believe."

"Well, maybe that worked when you were in the White House, but today the world is much more complicated."

"You're right, it is more complicated. But certain principles still apply—at least for me."

"I can't appeal to your patriotism?"

"I am a patriot. And, may I remind you, I got killed for my belief in the Union—as did so many hundreds of thousands of others. I just think you're far too focused on what will make your boss look better today and tomorrow. Trust me, if I say nice things about the TPP, we'll all suffer in the long run. History will mock us all. And now I'm done talking about this part of the subject."

Patchett was clearly stunned at having his orders ignored. When he tried to dominate, he was full of energy. Now he seemed depleted as he negotiated a "compromise" with Linc, which was exactly what Linc wanted all along.

Patchett left and Linc went back to reading. At 10:00 the entourage from the *New York Times* arrived. The sight stunned us. Two reporters, a photographer, and then four Lincoln experts trooped in one by one. Presumably, the *Times* wasn't completely swayed by DNA evidence. The four were Doris Kearns Goodwin, who had won the Pulitzer Prize for her Lincoln book, *Team of Rivals*; Stephen B. Oates, who had written a Lincoln biography and many other Civil War-era books; James M. McPherson, who had won the Pulitzer for *Battle Cry of Freedom*; and, finally, Harold Holzer, a casual friend of Dad's who had written dozens of books about Lincoln, making him perhaps more responsible than any other living individual for getting that Lincoln book total to 15,000.

Oh, how I wanted to be in the room with the reporters, historians, and Linc. Instead, one of the reporters came out of the dining room and sat us all down in the family room so he could write a feature on the folks who had taken in Abe Lincoln. That the paper would choose this angle for a story was obvious—so obvious it had never occurred to me. I was so focused on helping Linc with research, then trying desperately to convince him not to select the beach/shuffleboard option, that I had completely forgotten our family's role in the whole enterprise.

After forty-five minutes, the reporter rejoined the closed-door meeting with Linc. Four and a half hours later, the interview ended and they emerged. The historians looked a bit dumbfounded, a slightly milder version of the disorientation Dad had showed when he first saw Linc. Dad pulled Harold Holzer aside and asked what he thought.

"Absolutely amazing," Holzer said. "He's the real deal. And your son found him in Central Park? That's quite a coup for the Mason family. Jack, all I can say is, I wish it had happened to me. By the way, do you think the three of us could grab a cup of coffee at some point?"

Dad said maybe, but he wasn't sure there would be enough time. But he promised to call Holzer the next day because he wanted his advice. And then we all went up to Linc as the interview team filed out. I wanted to ask him how it had gone, but couldn't find the right words. Dad came to the rescue with a one-word query.

"Well?" he said.

"Very stimulating," Linc said. "There were some smart people in that room, and the reporters let the historians ask some questions. They also asked me about Seward and the Gettysburg Address and a lot about General McClellan. The reporters wanted to know if I'd be a Democrat today."

"What did you say?" Dad said.

"I said the Democratic Party was horrible in 1860—it was for slavery and against internal improvements and a national bank— and "I know from experience that parties can change radically over time. Both major parties are equally unrecognizable to me today. So I refused to answer. I said any answer I gave would only be a distraction. I believe in climate change because I've looked at the evidence. It's not because I've emerged as a Democrat after all those years of hibernating as a Republican."

"Did they like your plans for the Lincoln Foundation?" I said.

"They were very interested and respectful, but no one seemed certain we could implement the ideas. We shall see."

He paused. "Henry, I need a break. Can we go to Starbucks?"

Chapter 8

WE WALKED THERE almost without speaking. I took my lead from Linc, who might have felt all talked out after being grilled for more than five hours. Finally, he spoke.

"Your father showed me something very interesting that Gore Vidal wrote about me. He seems very smart, and I should like to meet him."

"Well, he's dead."

"So am I most of the time."

"Indeed. I'd love to help, but I think you'll have to work on the scheduling, Linc."

"You know what I'd like to do when we get back?" he said. "Watch some more tapes of the presidential candidates. It's time to meet the porter in *Macbeth*. We need some comic relief."

We spent the rest of the day working. Then, after dinner, we watched the candidates some more. We saw Crockenstock begin to weave a new theme into all his speeches, the "fact" that representatives of the media were among the most loathsome creatures on the planet. "They're truly terrible, ugly people—most of them anyway. They peddle lies all the time."

Ah, this campaign was getting truly surreal. Perhaps the biggest liar in American political history was telling preemptive lies about reporters by calling them—what else?—liars. "This must be his strategy to inoculate himself against some devastating print pieces he knows will come eventually," Dad said.

And then there was Senator Arrogandez trying to one-up Crockenstock by promising to torture our enemies for twenty-seven days before boiling them in the oil he intended to steal.

"This is how modern politics works," Dad said. "Your opponent says something horrible and disgusting, but the crowd cheers wildly. So you then feel obligated to say something more horrible and more disgusting. And so it goes, around and around."

"That Arrogandez is a real zealot," Linc said. "I'd hate to break bread with him."

Alas, we all agreed. I'm not sure Linc got the comic relief he craved. But it was too late to worry about that. At precisely 10:00 p.m., our two landlines and four cell phones all rang. The *New York Times* had posted its stories online.

"Time for a selfie now of me and President Lincoln?" Livvie said. We said sure.

We had no time to read the stories as we tried desperately to answer all the calls. The first wave came from agents, book publishers, and TV producers. A few of the publishers mentioned specific dollar amounts, but most just begged us not to accept a deal with anyone else until they got back to us with a firm offer in the morning.

It was chaos. Mom and Livvie were on the phone in the family room, Dad and I took the one in the kitchen. Linc went from one to the other to listen to the different offers on speaker.

Overcome by enthusiasm, or something, one publishing executive promised to turn Abraham Lincoln into "a household name." Dad and I thanked her, then politely suggested the nation had beaten her to it by many years. Undeterred, she said, "But I mean *today.*" We did not put her on the list of people we'd get back to in the morning.

Livvie came in to tell us the producer of a cheesy TV talk show took a very different tack. "He said having President Lincoln on 'would be almost as big a thing as when Jay Z and Beyoncé were on together to deny the divorce rumors.'"

"That guy's priorities are really warped."

Hard to argue with that. "But at least he's honest," I said. Then I laughed. If we decided to go cheesy, he might well be our first call.

"Oh, my God," Livvie shouted. "Get over here now. Look out the window."

We opened the curtains some more and then saw that hundreds of people, or maybe thousands, had gathered on the sidewalk outside our building. I had been casually thinking that Linc's return was the biggest story since the moon landing, but now I was starting to grasp that many would see it as the biggest story ever. Dad called the police. Within minutes several squad cars had arrived and officers had set up barricades outside our building and were standing guard, providing some semblance of crowd control.

Mom collapsed on the sofa and Dad went into the kitchen to make some tea. "Jack, I'm going to need a major foot rub."

My cell rang. I had been waiting for this call. It wasn't a dumb agent or producer. It was Josh. "Dude, why didn't you say something? I can't believe my best friend is hosting Abe Lincoln!"

I felt as if I'd been upgraded from coach to business class. I apologized for misleading him earlier.

"It's not as if you did a good job of it," he said. "I knew something was up, I just had no idea what. I mean, Livvie home to do homework? C'mon. I know I should have guessed that Abraham Lincoln had come back, but I didn't. I was thinking of something a little smaller. So what happens now—and when can I meet him?"

I told him we were fielding offers and that I thought he could come by after school tomorrow.

"Will you be in school?" he asked.

"I have not thought about that for one second." And that was true. I was too absorbed in our Linc project.

"Gillian might be impressed," he said. "Your picture looked good in the story."

Right. I had forgotten about the sidebar they did on my family.

"Tempting, very tempting, but if she's going to be impressed for only one day, then rushing to see her doesn't seem like a great idea. Besides, I want her to like me for me."

"Bullshit."

"No, no, not bullshit. I speak truth. At least I think I do."

Just then call waiting said headmaster Elmore Mastiff was on the line. It was already 10:30 and I really wasn't expecting any more calls. "Josh, Master Mastiff is calling. I think I need to take it."

"Gee, now what could be on his mind? Does he often call you at home, Henry? Are you the headmaster's pet?"

"Eat me, Josh. Bye."

Josh and I called Mastiff His Royal Shakedown because, no matter what was going on, he always seemed to be fund-raising. Good news provided a ready excuse to beg for money, as did bad news. And no news. I felt for the guy, sort of. And now, I was about to learn, he was ready to put the arm on me.

"Henry," he said, "we think it would be wonderful if President Lincoln could spend an hour or two with the board of trustees and Forbish Milton's other big donors. It would help the school so much. You know, you're already a very valued member of the Forbish Milton community. Very valued."

Actually, I didn't know that. And I didn't feel that—until I met a certain guy with a beard in Central Park.

Something felt wrong. I started fidgeting like crazy. I didn't know why, but I didn't want to comply. "President Lincoln will be so busy trying to reform politics that he might not have time to get to Forbish Milton."

"I'm sure you could make time, Henry. The school would be very grateful. This could even have an impact on your grades."

Oh my God. "But I get As now." In fact, it was my A in history that allowed me to retain dining privileges in my father's home.

"Well, there is always next year to be concerned about. Or we could find a way to get your family some scholarship money. I'm sure we could do something that would help convince you. There might even be a way to see that Mr. Newsome does not finish his term as eighth-grade president."

My brain froze. Was my little academic world every bit as slimy as the worst parts of politics? Tonight it seemed to be.

"Master Mastiff, I will look into this, but I still think it won't be possible. For now, let's pretend this conversation never took place."

"You may be making a terrible mistake, Henry. A very, very, very terrible mistake."

He had used three "verys," which suggested I might be in some very deep shit. I started to think that for no good reason I had angered a man who had a lot of power over me. Master Mastiff had a once-in-a-lifetime chance to be a hero in the eyes of his biggest donors, and I had snatched that away from him. "Think it over," he said, before we ended the call.

Whenever I had a political problem, I went straight to Dad. When he got off the phone with the producer of *Ellen*, I told him what had happened.

He put his hand on my shoulder. "I know you know this, but I want to be absolutely clear. We don't get a penny from anything that happens with President Lincoln. It would be wrong. It would dishonor him—and us. Your headmaster is trying to help your school, but he's also trying to help himself."

"How can I still go to Forbish Milton after this?"

"We'll talk about that after President Lincoln is gone. For now, you did the right thing. I'm proud of you, Henry. You do the right thing almost all the time. Most parents can't say that about their thirteen-year-olds."

"Thanks, Dad."

In the midst of all the calls, Mom had decided on a slight change in media strategy. She booked Linc on *The Today Show*, *Good Morning America*, and *CBS This Morning*. We knew they would all ask which party he would be in now and what he had to say about the afterlife. We told Linc he'd then be allowed to say whatever he wanted about reforming the political system.

The calls stopped around 11:00, and we were finally able to read the *New York Times* coverage. In one sidebar, the four historians explained their different reasons for believing that this Abe Lincoln was genuine. Professor Holzer even said that Linc sounded the way he probably did in 1865. The main story took Linc's proposed reforms very seriously, as did two op-ed columns by *Times* regulars.

We were all pleased. "Well, Olivia, Debra, Jack, and Henry," Linc said, "the *New York Times* seems to know why I am here, which is a good thing. They didn't always feel that way when I was president. The founder and editor, Henry Raymond—another Henry—was sometimes my friend and sometimes a very stern critic. But he meant well, which cannot be said of every man."

Mom prepped Linc on compressing his answers to fit the four- to ten-minute slots the morning shows were giving him. He got the hang of it pretty fast. "If your client were the loquacious Secretary Henry Seward," he said, "you'd probably be pulling your hair out by now."

Then we had tea in the family room. "So, Mr. President, how do you feel?" Dad said.

"I feel what I am saying may actually get heard. That's much of what I could ask. What I can't possibly assess is how people will react to the fact that the message is coming from me, a president who died so long ago."

"We don't want to overschedule you," Mom said. "How many writing offers should we accept?"

"I appreciate all the kind things you have said about me as a writer, but don't forget one thing. I am a slow one. I am accustomed—was accustomed—to laboring over every word. But I've done a lot of thinking in the last few days, and I certainly believe I can write one book in the time I have left. And I will follow Olivia's suggestion to write letters to the billionaires who might want them. Excuse me, but it is still difficult for me to imagine that someone could have accumulated so much money. I surely don't know how the world works anymore if even that idiot Crockenstock can amass a billion dollars.

"When I was young, the richest man in America was John Jacob Astor, who first made his money in fur trading, then made a second fortune in New York City real estate. I remember reading that in 1803 he bought a seventy-acre farm that ran from Broadway to the Hudson River between Forty-Second and Forty-Sixth Streets. I suspect it is a farm no longer. Then he bought a lot of land from Aaron Burr, who was living in disgrace after his duel with Alexander Hamilton.

"Thinking of Burr reminds me there were politicians with crazy ideas before the 2016 campaign for the presidency. Around the time I was born, Burr was determined to become King of Mexico. Not president, king.

"But I digress, oh do I digress. And I should not, because we have pay-toilet moguls and potentially catastrophic climate change to worry about."

"One reason I usually love my job," Dad said, "is that I am trying to show young people how fascinating American history is. And, in many ways, I believe the story has a happy ending, although these days we're all having our doubts about that. We are a somewhat dysfunctional democracy. At the moment, some prominent politicians sound as if they want to turn us into a theocracy, which would be a tragic end for the American experiment."

"Amen," Linc said, "unless that is an improper response."

Chapter 9

W E WOKE TO find that Linc's return was, naturally, the biggest news story in the world. Although this could have been predicted even by those who operated psychic hotlines, it was still a shock. We were living with the man and just going about our business of trying to help him, hour by hour. Talking to him every day had begun to feel normal. But the wall-to-wall news coverage of our little story no longer felt normal at all.

Journalists emphasized two points: a famous man had returned from the dead, and he came with an agenda that might improve our political system. Some pointed out that it was easier to believe in the first premise than the second.

We missed seeing how Linc and Mom would react to the candidates' responses because the two of them were away making the rounds of the network morning shows. Not surprisingly, the leading presidential candidates seemed to doubt that focusing on lying in politics was such a good idea. Before Linc appeared on any morning show, four candidates had done phone interviews on the *Morning Joe* TV show, which started at 6:00 a.m. Dad, Livvie, and I gathered in the family room to watch.

Crockenstock called in first. "First, consider the source of these remarks," he said. "This is an ugly, bitter man. He looks like a dead person. Hey, he is a dead person. He's an ugly zombie who's bitter about being dead so he tries to cut down people like me who are good-looking and successful and not dead. He's a loser.

"It's amazing that anyone says anything good about this guy, because from everything I've read, he was a complete disaster with women. He never got any good women, and when he did finally find someone who would marry him, she turned out to be a crazy person. She probably went crazy because she had to look at him every day. The man is hugely overrated."

"But he freed the slaves and led the North to victory in the Civil War," Mika Brzezinski said.

"I would have won the war sooner and freed the slaves much earlier. I could have ended the war in three months, maybe two. It's all about management."

"That would have saved a lot of lives and saved historians a lot of time," Dad said. "The more he yaps, the more outrageous he gets. He has no limits."

"But what about his charge that you lie all the time?" said Joe Scarborough.

"Tiny ugly men with small minds get all excited about this truth thing. When you dream big, as I do, you sometimes get a little carried away by the grandeur of your ideas. So that sometimes puts you in an exaggeratory posture, or even in the realm of the prevaricative. But it is rare that I go there, and when I do go there I know it is for the right reasons, as a service to society.

"And then there is this. How can a man who says he never told a lie have the temerity to try to regulate the other half of public speech, the inventive half, when, by his own admission, he claims to be totally ignorant of it? This makes no sense. And do you realize that the First Amendment does not include the word 'truth'? Branding someone a liar can only inhibit free speech and is probably a violation of the

First Amendment. The Supreme Court has long talked about the value of the free exchange of ideas in the marketplace. Even fake ideas have their place. False statements allow true statements to shine more brightly, so they have greater intellectual value. Take away the false statements and the true statements wouldn't look so good. One could almost argue that, in helping to highlight by contrast what is true, the false statements are actually more valuable than the true statements. So, obviously, nothing should be done to suppress them.

"Not that I make false statements. I do not. I merely embellish occasionally. But that is only because my good ideas are so colossal."

"I'm not sure children should be allowed to hear this," Dad said.

"So," said Scarborough, "what you're saying is that you don't lie, but that lies constitute highly beneficial speech?"

"Precisely. In fact, I think you could argue that liars are one of the most unprotected classes in the country. And I believe in standing up for them, as I do for all little people."

The next caller was Senator Arrogandez. "Because of my deep and abiding faith in the Lord, and His in me, you know that if I say something it will be the truth," he began. "It may not initially appear to be the truth—it may appear to be contradicted by what some people call, with evil intent, 'facts'—but since you know I can't lie, even what appears to be a lie will turn out to be the truth. I have prayed for guidance on this, and I have been told that I am the truth-teller. So, therefore, I am, regardless of what some godless ultraliberal committee of misfits may declare. Because I mean well, I cannot mislead, distort, deceive, defame, libel, or purvey disinformation in any way. Look into yourself, for it is your eyes that deceive. It is not me."

"I want to be sure you all understand this," Dad said. "The senator was saying it was the committee, which does not yet exist and has not as yet labeled anyone a Lincoln Liar, that would be the guilty party if it ever labeled anyone a liar because it would be projecting the transgressions of its members onto poor patriots like Senator Arrogandez."

But the senator was not done. "Besides, this benighted committee would ignore the crucial issue of time. The zombie Abraham Lincoln said I was a man who scoffed at science, but this is not true. Einstein's special theory of relativity tells us that different observers at different points will experience different realities, so in that sense, something that is not true today may well be true in the future, and to certain observers, that future may already be here."

"Are you saying, Senator Arrogandez," said Brzezinski, "that a person who said man can fly in the nineteenth century was not lying because airplanes were subsequently developed in the twentieth century?"

"No, I am not saying that at all."

"Well, could you elaborate on what you are saying, then?"

"It should be obvious."

"It is not obvious to me."

"But the American people understand me."

Frankly, I am not sure they did. But I've got to hand it to Senator Arrogandez. It was brilliant of him to cultivate a reputation for being whip-smart since now, whenever voters found the logic of one of his pronouncements impenetrable, they assumed the fault lay not with him but with them. It is a rare talent, having people blame themselves for your bad ideas.

Nora Blitzen was next. Unlike the two gentlemen, she welcomed President Lincoln warmly, although she didn't understand what his emphasis on lying had to do with her. "I don't lie," she said. "I simply lose track of things for extended periods." Then she pivoted to discussing policy initiatives she believed "the late and now not-so-late president would favor."

Senator Plotnik was the next to speak. "President Lincoln was a great man, and perhaps the greatest thing he ever did was impose the first income tax on August 5, 1861. Now, I want to inherit his legacy and do more with the income tax than he ever dreamed possible."

Then it was time to watch Linc on TV. I was biased, of course, but I thought he did really well. He even used Livvie's line—"If your argument is so compelling, why do you have to lie?"—during each appearance. Livvie was thrilled. Justifiably. When Linc wasn't on air, we snuck into the kitchen to grab food and bring it back to the family room.

Asked for his view of Crockenstock, Linc called him "a silly, lying, racist fool, and perhaps the biggest horse's ass ever to seek the presidency. As a human being, he's an utter loser." And Senator Arrogandez? "He's a dangerous science denier and a religious zealot." And Nora Blitzen? "Oh, I had some notes about her, but I can't find them." And Senator Plotnik? "Like me, he believes in equal opportunity. But he may be a little too focused on equal outcomes for the country's good."

Naturally, Crockenstock went nuts afterwards. On a Fox News show, with spittle flying, he said, "Lincoln might have been the worst president we ever had. Two and a half percent of the U.S. population died because he couldn't avoid the war." He was so red and his eyes were bulging so much that he looked completely crazed. If someone had handed him a live chicken right then, he might have bitten its head off, circus-geek style. "Presidential" was absolutely the last word one would have used to describe his demeanor.

The turd mogul was so furious that he dragged his wife into the campaign for the first time. Exalta Crockenstock issued a press release stating that Abraham Lincoln was "a mean little smelly/ugly/beastly man, not the kind of man a gorgeous woman with perfect breasts and legs and buns of steel would ever want because of how he looks, the fact that he's dead, and because, in the 206 years since his birth, he has been unable to amass a respectable net worth. I ask you, what kind of man is that? Can he even be called a man?"

Linc wasn't happy when he returned. "The interviewers were very interested in the idea of lying in politics, but they largely ignored the fact that I wanted to focus on lying about climate change. And by the time I was about to return to the subject, they were saying 'Thank you and goodbye.' I have to take more command next time."

"You were once commander in chief," I said.

"So some people thought, if not others," Linc said.

Again, we split the family in half to work the phones as the offers began to pour in. We agreed to a $20 million book deal with Random House. But then a more obscure publisher rang and demanded to speak to Linc. He joined Dad and me in the kitchen and listened via speaker.

"I'm impressed that you were always so trim," he said, "even with the anxiety of the war hanging over you."

"Well, I hardly had the stomach to eat during the war," Linc said.

"Oh, that's great, that's great. You've just got to write *The Civil War Diet* book."

"Yes, I'll tell people that by not sleeping much and worrying yourself sick so that all food seems equally unpalatable, you too can lose weight."

"Not only were you a great president, but you are also a great pitchman. You outlined the premise brilliantly. This book could be enormous. We're ready to offer $4 million."

"There will be no such book," Linc said. "Doctors told me my Civil War diet was very unhealthy, so I'm not going to teach readers how they can become unhealthy as well."

"Okay, you're also a good negotiator. God, this guy is good at everything. No wonder he's number one with a bullet. I mean, never mind. Instead of the four mil advance, let's make it five. But that's as high as I can go."

"Sir, I am not negotiating. I am saying no. Take your offer, put it between two slices of bread, and eat it. Enjoy. That's my dietary tip for you."

"The man talks in one-liners. He's beyond brilliant. Okay, okay. Six million dollars."

"Which button do I press to get rid of him?"

We both pointed. "Ah, I like technology," Linc said.

Moments later Livvie had another reason to smile. Allergan, the maker of Botox, called to offer Linc $50 million to be the brand's public face. Of course we said no, but we were all impressed that Livvie had nailed the number precisely. "Way to go, Livvie," Mom said. On some subjects, Livvie was a whiz.

The next $50 million offer came from LinkedIn. Who knew a bad pun could be worth so much? We said yes. All Linc had to do was write a few paragraphs about the importance of meeting the right people. Nice work if you can get it.

Dad then got a strange text saying that rival congressmen had introduced two extraordinary bills. Clearly, the lunacy President Lincoln's return inspired seemed bipartisan. One bill stated that if your second term were cut short by assassination and you came back from the dead, term limits would not prevent you from seeking a third term. The other bill sought to ban all public utterances by zombies. The bill would create a national commission to determine who was a zombie and who was not, a power that, opponents pointed out, could be abused. In less than an hour, the bill garnered 135 cosponsors. President Obama responded by saying the bill would be "dead on arrival."

Then a surprisingly conciliatory Lee Patchett of the White House called. Could Linc meet with President Obama and all the surviving presidents at the White House on Sunday? Of course. Mom volunteered to take Linc.

We set up the *60 Minutes* show, a two-hour special to be taped on Saturday, and the Cooper Union speech, as well as a special with Oprah Winfrey. Then Fox News called. We listened and said we'd call back.

We then explained Fox News to Linc, which wasn't easy. "They would represent the most hostile media environment you would face," Dad said. "They have a right-wing view of everything, and their interviewers do not believe humans cause climate change. And the network absolutely despises President Obama. Having said that, you would have the opportunity of reaching some voters you wouldn't get to otherwise. And there's probably no risk in doing it. So it's up to you."

"Ah," said Linc, "I feel my vanity rising once again, given that I always felt that if I could actually talk to a person I had a chance of bringing them over to my side. Let's say yes."

And so we did.

Then the Beacon Theatre, one of the city's top rock 'n' roll venues, called to invite Linc to do a two-hour "town hall." We agreed to the same tiered pricing strategy—a range of $50 to $50,000—that would be employed by Cooper Union.

Then George, our super, buzzed us. I answered. "Mr Henry, there is a big crowd of your neighbors in the lobby. They are waiting to see President Lincoln. Could someone come down and talk to them? Also, the crowd outside is enormous and noisy, and some of your neighbors are terrified. There are people camping out in a line that goes all the way to the East River."

When I got to the lobby, I was shocked. At least fifty of my neighbors had crammed into the small space, and there were thousands of people outside. I suddenly felt like the parent about to say there would be no ice cream today.

"President Lincoln is busy working on various projects to help fund his foundation. He would love to come down to say hello, but he can't right now."

Some people sighed, others groaned. Mrs. Maggert just glared.

"I know you're disappointed, but he won't be seeing you today. I'm sorry. I'll let you know the next time he is leaving the building so you can meet him."

When I got back upstairs, Dad showed me a bizarre, but somehow predictable, news item stating that three men in different parts of the country were claiming they had predicted Lincoln's return.

"Really?" I said. "On this day? This year?"

"Religious nuts have been predicting the end of the world for centuries," Dad said, "giving chapter and verse on exactly when it would happen. As usual, hundreds of desperate, damaged people are flocking to these Lincoln 'prophets' and joining their cults. Interestingly, two of the 'prophets' said their followers will be assured a wonderful afterlife in a special part of heaven known as Lincolnia."

"Is that where you've been hanging out?" I asked the most likely resident of that territory.

"Even I didn't get to go there, as far as I know," Linc said. Then it was time for Mom to take him to the *Hannity* and Oprah tapings.

The phone rang, and Dad told me I had a call from Marshall Wendell. I said I'd take it on the extension in my room. Wendell was an obnoxious billionaire hedge fund manager who was head of the board of trustees at Forbish Milton. Can you guess the nature of his call?

"You know," he said, "you could really help yourself if you made President Lincoln available to some of the school's biggest donors."

"I don't think there will be time," I said.

"You could be a big hero if you could bring him to school."

"I would love to, but his time is so limited and there is so much he needs to do. I don't think he was sent here to help fund-raise for my school."

"I think that would be one of the very best things he could do. You do believe in education, don't you?"

"I do."

"Well, if you refuse to help your school better educate its students, things might not go so well for you at school."

"What might happen?"

"Some of your As might turn into Bs—or worse."

Where had I heard this before?

"So you're threatening me?"

"I'm just suggesting that if you're smart, you'll choose the right path. It would be so easy for you to do. And I would really appreciate it. Let me tell you a little story. My son Harlan is a year ahead of you at Forbish Milton. Last year he was getting straight As—except in English, where he had a B+. So I spoke to his teacher, and we went back and forth, and finally I said, 'I give a lot of money to this school, and I really think you should consider changing his grade or you might need to look for another job.' Long story short, he changed Harlan's grade. I usually get what I want."

"Is it fun being so corrupt?"

"You're making a mistake. In investing, as in tennis, we call what you're doing an unforced error." He was so certain that he was right and that he would prevail over an insignificant little pipsqueak like me that it was infuriating.

"I know you get your way almost all the time, but you really don't want me for an enemy. I'm Abe Lincoln's friend."

"Whoop-dee-doo. Look, son, you just don't seem to get it. I'm a winner. I always win. Remember that. Do you really want to line up against someone like me? I certainly hope for your sake that you reconsider." In his view, I had just fired a spitball at his battleship. Nothing of consequence here. "I expect to hear from you tomorrow." And then he hung up.

Can you feel exhilarated and nauseated at the same time? Yes, apparently. Standing up to one of the titans of the city felt great, but what if there were awful consequences? When the adrenaline wore off, though, I simply felt sad. I realized this would absolutely have to be my last year at Forbish Milton.

Friends had been calling all day, so we spent a little time getting back to people. Then there was a batch of calls from agents, producers, publishers, business managers, and stockbrokers targeting members of the Mason family rather than our celebrated guest. They even made book offers to me. I took their numbers but said I had no immediate plans to do anything. I was busy.

"Well, when you change your mind—and you will—give me a call," one agent said.

We tried to unwind with a few minutes of TV. If one of the world's crazed leaders had been planning to start a war today, he'd probably reconsidered, figuring that Lincoln's return meant that even spectacularly gruesome massacres and world-class human rights abuses would get scant coverage. Judging from the non-Lincoln articles in the *Times*, the world seemed moderately peaceful on this day, at least by Earth standards.

As we channel-surfed, we noticed that some of the movie channels had gone wall-to-wall Lincoln—*Abe Lincoln in Illinois*, *Lincoln*, and even *Abraham Lincoln: Vampire Hunter*. Finally, we briefly played a DVD—*Naked Gun 2 ½: The Smell of Fear*—and just cracked up at the opening scene, ostensibly set in the George H. W. Bush White House. This was genuine comic relief, untinged by sadness for our country.

Linc and Mom returned around 4:00. "My treatment by Mr. Hannity on Fox was abusive, nonsensical, unpleasant, and utterly mystifying," Linc said. "Just as your mother said it would be. She prepared me exceedingly well. And Miss Winfrey was lovely, as expected."

After a while, Dad caught my attention. "Henry, can I talk to you for a few minutes?"

I tensed immediately, like all kids knowing there was a great difference between shooting the breeze with a parent and having a formal sit-down. Had I done something terribly wrong? Was Dad having second thoughts about my decision to rebuff Forbish Milton? Or, good God, did he just realize he had left out some humiliating detail from last year's harrowing sex talk, which had left me wondering if a sex life could simply be outsourced? ("There's outcall, certainly," said Josh with his typical basso profundo authority. "Outsourcing, not so much. How would that work?")

Dad and I sat down in his small study. "I know how close you and President Lincoln are, and I don't want to step on your toes," he began, "but I was hoping to write a book about his return and some of the things we've learned. The book would be important for my career. Given how little I've written, I was lucky to get tenure when I did.

"As you know, I've thought for a long time about writing a Lincoln book. I've made quite a few false starts. It's been difficult. The more I wrote the more convinced I became that what I had to say wasn't new enough. The good news is that Lincoln is endlessly fascinating. The bad news is that he fascinates so many people. There are already so many books about him that I felt there was no room for whatever I had to say. Yet people in the department and the administration keep reminding me that I needed to deliver a Lincoln book."

Dad had never said a word of this before. So Josh was right all along. How could he have known?

"Well, now a Lincoln book seems to have fallen into my lap. But I know it fell into your lap first. Have you considered writing a book about our visitor?"

Dad seemed nervous asking the question, almost sex-lecture nervous. It hurt to see him so upset. It made me want to take care of him.

"Yes, sort of, but your book should absolutely come first. I don't have a career to worry about. That's a good thing, given what you've taught me about the history of child labor laws. There wouldn't be anything scholarly in my book. It would be more a kid's political adventures with an undead president."

"I think I can promise you the word 'undead' won't appear in my book—unless a publisher demands it. But I just want to be sure that nothing I do deprives you of what could be a great thing, whether or not you want to go into politics. You may not have a career, but you do have a life, and it's very precious to your mother and me."

"Thanks, Dad. I don't know how serious my political ambitions are. If Linc can't change the system at all, then I'm not sure I'd want to be part of it."

"So it's really okay with you if I go ahead with a book?"

"Absolutely. You are the history maven of the house, and you deserve it."

"Thank you, Henry. Thank you very much."

Letting my father write the first book seemed only fair, especially given how many hundreds of hours he had spent teaching me about history. I wanted to say that to him, but somehow I couldn't. I just hoped he understood. According to tradition, we concluded our session with an awkward hug. Once again, we'd had a heart-to-heart talk and both of us more or less survived.

As for politics, I meant what I'd said at our first dinner with Linc and I'd meant what I told Dad. Sure, it might be nice to be president—in a different world. That first night, I'd thought Linc might help create that new world. Now, three days later, nothing good had yet come of Linc's visit, and the broad, powerful river of political slime continued to flow. One crazed congressman wanted Linc to resume his presidency, while another thought we needed to create a tribunal to identify, and then silence, zombies. Meanwhile, two representatives of Forbish Milton had shown how deep corruption ran at my own little school. Why would a sane person assume it wasn't at least as bad in the wider, sleazier realm of politics where the stakes were much higher? Politics? Hmm, I just didn't know.

As I watched his appearance later that night, it was clear that Linc's casual attitude toward Fox News had quickly changed once he'd encountered Sean Hannity's singular world view.

"Great to have you," said Hannity. "Let's start by being honest. If you were alive today—I mean really alive—you would be a Republican, right?"

"I have refused to answer that question because I've seen how profoundly the parties can shift over time. The party I picked today might be totally different in two generations."

"So you're going to weasel out of that one. So much for your reputation for courage. A different question. Do you really think Obama has done a good job? Isn't it obvious that he has tried to destroy this country?"

Linc stiffened when he heard the question. And then he visibly seemed to change from genial guest to man on a mission.

"No. What is obvious to me is that you and your network have helped racists who want to destroy this president. You and your fellow hosts have repeatedly had guests on who say the president was not born in the United States and is a Muslim, not a Christian. Guests on your network have said this sixty times in recent years. And how many times have you or other interviewers challenged their lies? Precisely eight times. When someone tells an obvious lie and you do nothing about it, you are complicit in that lie. You may not be a racist, Mr. Hannity, but you and your network sometimes help the cause of racism, whether intentionally or not. The way you have treated this president is despicable and has helped polarize the country. I'm curious, how do you respond?"

Hannity looked somewhat startled, then quickly tried to defuse the issue. "First, I'm sure your numbers are wrong."

"They are not. Samuel Johnson said patriotism was the last refuge of a scoundrel, but from what I've seen lately in this country, I think bogus statistics are the last refuge of a scoundrel."

"Umm, we are at times merely a forum for people to express various views."

"If Crockenstock came on and said Canadians are all ax murderers, would you say anything? Or would he be entitled to his point of view just like your other guests?"

"Well, if his lies are so obvious, we wouldn't allow him on."

"The birthers' lies were that obvious, yet you allowed them on. And Crockenstock was one of the biggest birthers of them all. Crockenstock's other lies are that obvious, yet you allow him on almost daily, usually without a challenge. Why is that? This is precisely how racism gets traction in America, when prominent people—people like yourself, who have real power—turn a deaf ear to what is being said around them. Tell me, do you believe the president was born in America?"

"His supporters say he was."

"That's not a real answer. What do *you* think?"

"I guess he was, although he sure took a long time to release his birth certificate."

"Do you hear how your response is still full of doubt? Even today? And you've continued to make comments about his finding the Muslim call to prayer in Jakarta 'one of the prettiest sounds on earth at sunset.' Yes, he did say that in an interview with the *New York Times* in 2007, but you know very well how that will be taken by many of your viewers and listeners. It will reinforce their view that this president is somehow illegitimate. You may not be a birther but you continue to help the birther cause in your own way."

"I resent that."

"Well, I resent how you help spread fanaticism. Mr. Hannity, facts are facts, whether you are happy with them or not."

"Well, I thought this was going to be an interesting conversation, but I was wrong. I'm astonished you were ever a Republican."

"A lot has changed since 1865. Have you noticed?"

Hannity was starting to show a little concern that being upbraided by Linc might not be good for his brand. "Now, if you're going to get snide—"

"I only get snide when I encounter someone so unaware of his own bias. You absolutely have the right to oppose the president politically. But you keep encouraging those who oppose the president on racial or religious grounds."

"But race has nothing to do with this."

"I think race has a great deal to do with this. It is no accident that a majority of Crockenstock's supporters think President Obama is a Muslim and that many are fans of your network. I think I'll leave now and attend to more important things."

Linc, obviously exasperated, stood up.

"So you're not going to give me a fair chance to Hannitize you?

Well, if you want to be a coward and leave before we've had a proper discussion, so be it."

"Sir, I have tried to have a proper discussion here, but it does not seem possible. Do you really want to spend your life promoting racial hostility? Don't you care about your legacy?"

When Hannity didn't respond, Linc walked off the stage.

Linc's appearance on the Oprah special was remarkably different. Here, he resisted the host's attempts to brand him a god-like hero. Oprah greeted Linc with what may have been the longest hug of his life, and she fussed over him as if he were a favorite child. She gazed lovingly at him and said, "The life I've had would have been inconceivable without you."

"Miss Winfrey, you flatter me," he said. "It's too much. I must tell your viewers I am not the paragon they may think I am.

"In my 1858 debates with Senator Douglas, I said that whites should be superior to blacks and that the two races could never live in harmony. I regret saying that, but it was what I believed at the time. I didn't know any better. I was a creature of my time. I was a staunch opponent of slavery, but I held that view without knowing any black people.

"Only later, when I was president and came to know people like Frederick Douglass, did I realize that blacks and whites were equal. But even then I wasn't sure I could say it. The Emancipation Proclamation was, as you know, initially a part of military strategy. I didn't give a speech suggesting that blacks should have the rights of full citizenship, including the right to vote, until right after the Civil War had ended.

"I've been told that John Wilkes Booth was in the audience for that speech and that it confirmed his intent to kill me."

"But given the times you lived in, you behaved heroically toward black people."

"Did I? I'm proud of some of what I did, considering the times. But when I look around me now and see people like you and

President Obama, I feel I harbored racist attitudes far too long. For the longest time, I couldn't see our races coexisting. I should have seen the truth sooner.

"And when I see that so much discrimination continues so long after my death, I wonder if things would have been different if I had behaved differently."

"What if you had talked more about slavery as being the cause of the war?"

"I was afraid to lose the tenuous support of the people that I had."

"Do you think it would have made a difference if you could have said that the war was over oppression?"

"It might have. But there also would have been enormous risk. We might not have won. Yet seeing how history has unfolded, I wonder if what I did was the best I could have done. All I can tell you is that I thought it was the best I could do at the time."

So history has been more kind to Lincoln than he was to himself. Imagine that. How rare that must be for people who have held extraordinary power.

I told Linc he had done a good job with Hannity.

"Henry, unfortunately it's the same in every age. There are people who just have no interest in learning what the truth really is. You could show them in twenty different ways and they would still never acknowledge it. So, please, promise me one thing."

"Yes?"

"Keep your mind and your heart open. Feel free to change your views when you find new evidence. As I told Miss Winfrey, I changed my mind about black people. I wish I had done it sooner, although I'm not sure that I actually could have, given my lack of knowledge at the time.

"In some ways, I wish I could have a second chance to see what I could do."

"Linc, you still have time left on this second chance."

"And so I do."

Chapter 10

THE NEXT MORNING after breakfast, I asked Linc to follow me into Dad's study. It was a great place for heart-to-heart talks, after all.

"I want to talk to you about why I went into school politics." He sat down, indicating that I should too, and steepled his fingers. I took a deep breath and began.

"You see how some of the adults associated with the school have treated me. Well, one reason I ran for office was because I thought Forbish Milton had treated its alumni shabbily. From the 1960s to the 1980s, about sixty of the school's students were molested by teachers and staff. The school covered up the scandal—that, sadly, was the norm back then—and, when it finally exploded in large headlines two years ago, they refused to apologize to the victims or investigate the matter. That last indecency was not normal.

"The most victimized alumni would be unable to hear an apology anyway. In addition to molesting children, Peter Pulham, an English teacher, also somehow controlled them. He told them they could become great if they followed him, but that their lives would be worthless if they didn't.

"Eventually eight of his students killed themselves. Articles about Mr. Pulham said he bragged about his power over young boys. He was a serial killer who taught young students about Melville, glory, humiliation, and self-slaughter."

Linc put his hand to his chin and thought.

"I assume there is no legal recourse?" he said.

"There is none. He is protected by statutes of limitations. What drives me really crazy is that one of his former students struck it rich on Wall Street, bought him a large house, and decided to subsidize him for the rest of his life. Not only hasn't he been punished, it's as if he's been rewarded."

"Henry, do you think life is fair?"

"No, but it should be more fair than this."

"Granted, but isn't this merely an extreme example of life's unfairness? What power do you have to change anything?"

"At school, I apparently have no power. I can't get Forbish Milton to apologize. I mentioned the situation to Gruesome Newsome, the class president, but he told me to give it a rest. But now you're here. Now I could go see Mr. Pulham and tell him how awful he is, and I could have Abe Lincoln tell him the same thing."

"And how would that help his victims?"

"Well, it wouldn't really, but it might hurt Mr. Pulham, and it would certainly make me feel better."

"Remember I said I might give you some political advice?"

"Yes."

"Channel your energy—and your emotions—toward achievable goals. If this monster were still committing crimes, we would do everything possible to stop him. Is he?"

"I don't think so. He is supposedly a hermit."

"Then I think you should put your energy into acts that help many other people, not just Henry Mason."

"So you think I'm being selfish?"

"That's not your intent, but that's how it looks to me. Henry, beware of symbolic acts that please the spirit—or the voters—without accomplishing anything worthwhile. If you become a politician, you don't want to be that kind of politician. But if you do find a way to say publicly that your school is corrupt, that might bring about actual change."

So I decided to bag the idea and concentrate on my return appearance at school. Linc had asked Dad for a list of things readers might want to know about him. Dad dashed off an eight-page list, then had Harold Holzer come over for an hour to speak with Linc and drop off *his* list of questions. I figured that would keep Linc occupied for the day.

Josh and I arrived at school together and he showed me off as if I were a prize pig at the county fair—or perhaps his best friend (maybe I was now). People who normally ignored me came over to talk. They had endless questions about Linc and were envious of Josh, who was going to come over after school to meet him.

Best of all, Gillian sat next to me at lunch. In another of those life-in-a-trance moments, she said, "You know, I kind of liked you before you hooked up with Abe Lincoln."

"You did?"

"Yeah. You didn't know?"

"Well, kind of. No. I guess I didn't."

Henry, I said, you know how to talk. Stop fidgeting and talk.

"You know," I said, "sometimes it's hard to tell the difference between what you hope for and what you know. So would you like to get together sometime?"

"Sure. We could go to Starbucks and talk."

A few seats away, Josh was making obnoxious faces, parodying my attempt at courtship. I ignored him. I ignored everybody except Gillian.

"Okay. I took President Lincoln to Starbucks right after I met him. He liked his grande cinnamon dolce latte and said they should open more Starbucks."

She laughed. Oh, I liked her even more.

"Yeah, I laughed too and then he gave me this look that suggested it was really bad form to laugh at a dead person for being out of touch."

"Is he very sensitive about that?"

"Only a bit. To be fair to the guy, he did die while he was president, and for the last five years of his life, I doubt he ever saw someone laugh at him because he didn't know something. I imagine you get used to deference—not that I would know anything about such things."

"No one defers to you?"

"No, figuring out how to respond to excessive deference has not been my problem."

"That's what happens when you're thirteen. No one sucks up to you. And that sucks. Maybe we need a national Suck Up to an Adolescent Day."

"Now, that is a great idea." Not only was Gillian beautiful, but she also thought a bit like a guy and was easy to talk to. This could be really great.

"Well, President Lincoln really seems to like you."

"He seems to. I think some of it is because I'm about the same age as his son Tad was in 1865, and because I know a lot of history and Shakespeare for a thirteen-year-old. Lincoln spent many nights, before and after he became president, reading and reciting Shakespeare with his family and friends. I haven't had the heart to tell him people don't do that anymore."

"So what does it all mean, that he came back from the dead to meet Henry Mason?"

"Oh, I'm just the help. He came here with a mission and needed a sympathetic guide. It could have been a lot of people."

"But it was you."

"I'm very glad it was me. It's only the highlight of my entire life."

I wondered if I should bring up my political ambitions, such as they were? Would she be impressed? Ah, screw it, I'd bring it up because it was true.

"And you know, President Lincoln and I have discussed the idea of my seeking higher office."

"Higher than the vice-presidency of the eighth grade at Forbish Milton?"

"Well, forgive my grandiosity, but as exalted as the position is, I may not stop there."

"Can you imagine going into politics?"

"If President Lincoln helps make it less of a sewer, yes, I could. But only then. I'd like to make the world a better place, and, theoretically at least, politics can be a way to do that."

The bell rang for class.

"Anyway, I have to run to class, but can we go to Starbucks next week, after President Lincoln leaves?"

"Either during the week or maybe the weekend after this."

"Great. I really enjoyed talking to you."

And it was the truth. Gee, meeting Abe Lincoln and setting up my first date all in the same week. Maybe my life didn't suck after all.

As Josh and I headed home, I told him all about my Gillian conversation. "So, Henry, you may have a weekend date," he said. "A weekend date is special. If she weren't interested, she would never have mentioned the weekend. Are you going to bring a condom to Starbucks?"

"Josh!"

"Or tell her that if she wants to meet President Lincoln, well, you have certain physical needs?"

"Josh, I'm not going to turn the president into my wingman. It's bad enough he has to deal with Crockenstock and Arrogandez."

"Boy, he really drilled Crockenstock a new one on the *Today* show."

"A new asshole for the asshole. How fitting."

And then we were home and we found Linc in his bedroom, writing away. He looked up, saw us, and invited us in. And I felt this amazing warmth fill my chest, one of the most wonderful things I've ever felt. I was about to introduce my best friend to Abraham Lincoln. On the coolness scale, that was off the charts.

"So, young man, we have something in common. We both like Henry Mason."

"Yes. Is he treating you all right?"

"Very well, very well. He even takes me to Starbucks sometimes. And he gives me some good ideas. On that subject, is there anything that you think would help get young people more interested in the political process?"

"Maybe start a book club," Josh said. "Your foundation could recommend books that would help remind people what America is supposed to be and show readers what programs—whether public or private—actually make things better for people. Once you're gone, Henry could be the spokesman for that."

"Hmm, that's a good idea," Linc said. "It was a pleasure to meet you, but now I have to get back to work."

We went to my room. "Jesus," Josh said, "you didn't tell me he was going to quiz me. My God, he's just like your father."

"You gave a good answer, and thanks for nominating me to be a spokesmodel. It is a great honor."

"Don't mention it. You could be the spokesperson for unusual adolescents everywhere. But back to President Lincoln. If only more politicians were like him."

"How do we do that, exactly? Do we have time to try cloning?"

"Not sure that would work."

We kicked it around a bit without solving the problems of the world. Then we joined the rest of my family for a quick meal before we took Linc to the Beacon Theatre and his town hall meeting.

Chapter 11

LINC'S APPEARANCE AT the Beacon, an ornate, gilded former movie palace opened in 1929 on Broadway between Seventy-Fourth and Seventy-Fifth Streets, raised an interesting question. Who would introduce him? And that naturally raised a companion issue: What words would be adequate?

In the show biz sense, Abraham Lincoln was the ultimate man who needed no introduction. In the metaphysical sense, however, his appearance rather desperately needed an explanation no introducer was likely to have.

Given that, the organizers' choice was inspired. They selected Gail Collins, the *New York Times* op-ed columnist who was able to find humor in most situations and who came with a presidential pedigree, of sorts, having written a biography of William Henry Harrison, the president whose thirty-one-day tenure was the shortest on record.

We sat in the first row. I had been at the Beacon to hear Bob Dylan, Jackson Browne, Crosby, Stills & Nash, and Sara Bareilles. (I know, I'm so hip it's painful.) But we'd never had seats like these.

After a witty introduction, Linc came onstage from the wings, striding awkwardly as he always did when entering a room, sort of stomping his feet like a toddler who had just learned to walk. He sat down in a big chair and laid his arms on the arm rests. I heard some chatter and then some titters. And no wonder: Abe Lincoln was in the pose immortalized by his statue in the Lincoln Memorial.

As I looked to see some of the faces of the people laughing, I saw one familiar face that was not laughing. In fact, it was sneering. Ten seats away, also in the first row, was Senator Arrogandez. What was he doing here? He hated everything New York represented and wasn't bashful about saying so. Should we be worried?

I waved at Linc and he gave me a little smile, but then, like someone hamming it up in some awful sitcom, I desperately directed his attention to my left. He gave a little frown to convey a lack of understanding, but then his gray eyes kept moving and—aha!—he saw the senator. He nodded once in my direction but gave no clue what he thought about this surprise guest.

Then Linc came up to the podium. "Ladies and gentlemen, thank you for coming tonight. I see a distinguished surprise guest in the audience, Senator Fred Arrogandez of Louisiana."

The crowd booed lustily. We were on the Upper West Side, a place where people could live for decades without ever encountering a Republican, unless you happened to run into Joe Scarborough, who did actually live in the neighborhood.

"Please, please, such a response is inappropriate. The senator is an elected public servant who loves his country." You would never have known that Linc already hated his guts. "Senator, after I take an hour's worth of questions from the audience, would you like to come up and debate some issues with me?"

"I'm not dressed for it," the tieless senator said.

"Granted, you're not up to my fashion standards," Linc said. The audience laughed. "Hmm, I heard the same laughter when I held public office."

"Okay," said Senator Arrogandez.

"Folks, you're in for an interesting night. The senator was a champion debater in high school and I have had some debate experience myself, so I hope this will prove illuminating. But first, your questions."

Linc fielded the audience's questions adroitly, avoiding any chance to demonize those with opposing views. And he got some tough questions. Clearly, Senator Arrogandez was not the only Republican on the Upper West Side on this Friday night. Several questioners suggested Linc's reform agenda would be tainted by his "liberal" bias. Others worried that any bipartisan committee that recommended reading materials or liar labels would either be badly politicized— or hopelessly deadlocked—in the current take-no-prisoners political climate.

After an hour, Linc gestured to Senator Arrogandez. "Can we get a podium and microphone for the senator?" he said.

Senator Arrogandez shook hands with Linc, who cast a benevolent smile upon him as if he were a true friend—or a tasty dinner. Once he had a microphone, Senator Arrogandez said, "It will be nice to be in a debate that actually allows me more than a minute at a time to speak."

"I've seen some of the debates, and I know what you mean. As for me, it is nice to be able to debate at all, anywhere. Senator, to begin, you seem horrified by the size, indeed almost the very idea, of the federal government. Can you explain your view?"

"Yes. Most people in Washington, especially Democrats, but not exclusively Democrats, think the solution to every problem should begin and end with government. But relying on the federal government is usually ineffective, and it is always expensive. I believe it is better to tackle problems at the state and local level."

"Where I get confused, Senator, is when you say that many of your political opponents actively want to make the government bigger, as if they think bigger is better."

"They do think this way. Part of this is habitual. They see a problem and immediately think the federal government should take the lead. But the problem is also political. We have a Democrat in the White House, but most of the nation's governors and state legislatures are Republican. So this administration and its supporters have a bias against seeking solutions at the local level because they think they may not like the solutions they get."

"That I can follow, but then you say that the driving force behind the fight against global warming is a desire to expand the federal government."

"The biggest promoters of the bogus climate change theory are the people who would love to have the government expand to try to solve this problem, which, if you look at data for the last seventeen years, really doesn't seem to be a problem."

"But 1998 was the hottest year in modern human history because of an El Niño effect, according to certain satellite data. The year 2014 was actually hotter, according to most other sources. And 2015 is likely to be hotter still. The last decade has been the hottest in recorded human history no matter how you measure it. There is a clear warming trend over the last two centuries, and climate scientists project temperatures will keep rising in the future."

"Scientists thought temperatures would rise for the past seventeen years and they didn't. Mr. President, I must ask you, don't you find it odd that a man of the nineteenth century is telling people of the twenty-first century how they should think about a specific scientific issue?"

"I find it monumentally odd. You cannot imagine how bizarre I find it. But I also feel I have no choice but to say what I think. Now, Senator, let's broaden the topic just a bit. I think you see conspiracies where most people, myself included, simply see policy differences. You may be suffering from an excessively strong sense of narrative. You have this powerful belief in how the world works, and when the facts don't fit, you dispense with the facts and keep the narrative. This is not the way I would want to encounter the world as the leader of a nation.

"Either climate change is a problem or it is not. You need to analyze the issue with eyes wide open, without bringing in theories about suspected government aggrandizement. You need to talk to different kinds of scientists. You don't need to spend hours talking to oil company executives about global warming. Here, I'll save you time. Most don't believe in it. It's in their short-term economic interest not to believe in it and to convince as many important people as they can—people like yourself—that it is a hoax.

"Although I disagree with their position, I sympathize with them. Just as I sympathized with people who had inherited a plantation run by slave labor in my day. The abolitionists were telling them to give up their slaves and become moral men and women, but not offering them a dollar of compensation for making the change. Become moral and starve! Had I been a slaveholder, I don't think I would have selected the starvation option so quickly either. You can't understand anything about politics unless you analyze self-interest, and you also have to understand that intelligent people will try mightily to cloak their self-interest with pseudoscience, testimonials, and moralizing. Many eminent Southerners didn't merely defend slavery; they argued that it provided the ideal living conditions for black people. Freeing them from bondage, they said, might not only be bad for white people—especially white women—it would be terrible for black people."

"But the scientists pushing climate change doctrine are paid advocates of a liberal position."

The crowd booed.

"Actually, my friend Henry looked into that, Senator. The vast majority are academics who don't get grant money from an entity with a stake either in the fossil fuel industry or the renewable energy industry. In fact, it is the people who attack them who are generously funded by ExxonMobil, Shell Oil, and the Koch brothers. One individual oil man has already given your campaign $50 million. So much from one man? And I wonder what he thinks of climate change. These companies and individuals try to do what is best for their shareholders and themselves, not what is best for the country or the planet. And as for the candidates they fund, such as yourself, I think a German proverb captures the essence precisely: 'Whose bread I eat his song I sing.'

"Senator, I wish I had $51 million to give you. Then you might sing my song. Sorry, if I had $51 million, I don't think I'd give it to you."

Linc got a big laugh.

"And there's another problem in listening to these people to the exclusion of others. In my experience, no one can match the arrogance of rich businessmen. It's as if some of them have concluded that they must be very, very smart, because, were this not so, then why has the world seen fit to reward their labors so prodigiously? Need we look further than your rival Crockenstock for confirmation? And Lord protect you from the businessman who has had not one giant success, but two or three or four! Then these people just know for sure that they are always right and, furthermore, that they could solve all the nation's problems if only someone would let them. These are precisely the people whose motives—and intelligence—you should suspect.

"One of the differences between you and me is the degree of certainty and constancy in our politics. Given how you view climate change data, I'm not sure anything would ever change your mind. So let me ask, Senator, what would alter your views?"

"Some evidence."

More boos.

"Really? There is already overwhelming evidence. What kind of evidence are you referring to?"

"A sustained rise in temperature."

"Well, global temperatures have risen 1.5 degrees Fahrenheit in the last 135 years. Today, ninety-nine of the one hundred largest glaciers on the planet are shrinking. This melting ice has caused sea levels to rise substantially. Residents of many island nations are fighting desperately to prevent their beachfront property from being swallowed up by the sea."

"There are always floods, Mr. President. There are always droughts."

"Your stance would be more credible if less of your campaign money came from the fossil fuel sector."

"Well, President Lincoln, I do represent the state of Louisiana."

"Sir, if the correlation is as direct as that—if you represent a big fossil fuel energy state and therefore get a huge amount of money from that industry—in the new era of climate change, perhaps we cannot afford to have national officeholders who come from Louisiana, Texas, and North Dakota—or any other states where their representatives' allegiance can be so simply purchased. Sir, what is the chance that those who believe that human activity causes climate change are right and you are wrong?"

"Zero." Some in the audience gasped. Others threw tomatoes at the senator. Two went splat near his legs, soiling his pants. One just missed his head.

"Please, please," Linc said. "Even though I believe the senator is dead wrong, this is not an appropriate response. Show some respect."

"Thank you, Mr. President," said Senator Arrogandez.

"Now back to our discussion. Senator, I assure you, the chances are *not* zero. And I don't think America can afford to have a leader at this moment who thinks they are. I know you're smart in many ways, but your answer betrays what I think may be a willful ignorance of probabilities. Many climate scientists say it is already too late to avoid some of the baneful impacts of global warming.

"Let me put to you a question I've heard from two intelligent people. Given your gift for speaking and your impressive academic pedigree, they wonder whether you actually believe the things you say about climate change. Even if the virtually unanimous scientific consensus turns out to be wrong, it's hard to imagine the U.S. government not at least taking the threat seriously and acting, given that the penalty for not acting and being wrong is so grave. Because your opinion seems so narrow-minded and uninformed, they suspect you are simply saying things that will please your donors and a fairly radical group of voters."

"I believe every word I say."

"Sir, if you are wrong about climate change and you are elected president—"

"I like half of that hypothetical."

"What system would you have in place for learning that you are indeed wrong and have been misled by the fossil fuel industry? If I may speak from my own experience, when the frenzy of secession followed my election as president, I did at least consider alternatives to a civil war. Initially, I had grave doubts about going to war. Based on my own experience and what I have read, I want a president who at least entertains some doubt about his or her most important decisions.

"Senator, do you know the expression, 'God helps those who help themselves'? It is not in the Bible, but I always found it helpful nonetheless."

"I know it."

"I believe in God, sir, but during the Civil War I never felt I could relax because God favored our side. Obviously, religious Confederates felt God was on their side. It has been ever thus. And long ago I said that, in such a conflict, both sides could be wrong about God's allegiance. It seems to me that your faith has made your mind less energetic than it might be, that you are ignoring a potential peril either because you expect the Lord to do all the hard work or because you are doing the bidding of your donors or because you lack imagination. Do you think that God always solves man's problems?"

"When man is led by the righteous, the answer is yes. As is said in the Book of Matthew, 'Behold the fowls of the air: for they sow not, neither do they reap, nor gather into barns; yet your heavenly Father feedeth them. Are ye not much better than they?'"

"You quoted the gospel perfectly, but I shudder at the meaning you take from those words. I am reminded of Antonio's speech in *The Merchant of Venice*:

'The devil can cite Scripture for his purpose.
An evil soul producing holy witness
Is like a villain with a smiling cheek,
A goodly apple rotten at the heart.
O, what a goodly outside falsehood hath!'

"You smilingly tell us that the Lord will make everything all right for the faithful. I know from experience that faith is not enough. I believe the Lord expects more from us.

"Tell me, when do you think the earth was created?"

"I'm not a scientist."

"You are emphatically not a scientist, sir." The crowd laughed. Two more tomatoes landed harmlessly on the stage. "That you announced your candidacy at Liberty University, which teaches that the earth was created five thousand years ago and that the theory of evolution is false, seems at least a tacit endorsement of those positions. Do you care to comment?"

"No."

"If the earth was created five thousand years ago, your God really has had to work much harder than my God because he has had so much less time to do everything. And if you are right, wherever did your beloved fossil fuels come from? I would have thought they came from fossils. But it takes quite a while for buried matter to turn into oil or natural gas. You are aware, my dear senator, that there is incontrovertible evidence that the earth is billions of years old?"

"Some secular humanists say so."

"Hmm. We didn't have that term when I was around. Excuse me, I have to adjust my thinking for a moment. I don't want to beat this to death, but it is obvious to me that future leaders of this great country should harness the power of science in any way they can to improve life for all Americans. I signed the law in 1863 establishing the National Academy of Science to give the president good advice about science. Why would you ignore science? What is gained by doing so?"

"Science—or what is called science—has been so politicized that you can't trust the people who are pushing science. They have an agenda. It is one that, at times, I do not believe is in the best interest of the people of the United States. I think part of the president's job is to decide when such advice should be heeded and when it should not be."

"But if you come into the job with a strong bias that God will provide for this nation and for the planet, you may overlook important things *you* can do. Climate change is the most important issue of the day—it is your slavery—and we cannot afford to have candidates who are bought and paid for by the fossil fuel industry. The French ambassador recently said that the only group of citizens on the entire planet who doubt climate science is the Republican Party in the U.S. Congress."

"There always have to be pioneers. People like Galileo, Copernicus, and Newton. And we are pioneers in this."

"So you're pioneers in doubting science?"

"Yes."

"That's an interesting concept. Tell me, will your science advisers be science people or religious people?"

"Religious science people."

"That is also interesting, considering that in one survey 93 percent of the members of the National Academy of Sciences said they do not believe in God."

"That's their loss."

"But why is that number so skewed? Have the secular humanists taken over the National Academy of Sciences?"

"Apparently."

"Okay, Senator, let me try to move to a different topic. And again, it's related to the tension I sometimes see in today's world between the most religious Christians, on the one hand, and those who follow other faiths or no faith at all. You've used some pretty harsh words to describe people who disagree with you on spiritual or, for that matter, political matters. You have said that no Muslim or atheist should ever be president of the United States. This view of yours is clearly unconstitutional. Sometimes when I hear you speak, you make me think more of Torquemada, the leader of the Spanish Inquisition, than Galileo. So I must ask you, how inclusive would an Arrogandez presidency be?"

"First, I'd like you to consider the piano," Senator Arrogandez began. "To play, you need both the white keys and the black keys, and you need them working together. Everything must be harmonious. Complaining leads to disharmony. The white keys shouldn't complain about the black keys, and the black keys shouldn't complain about the white keys."

"That's totally stupid!" yelled a man.

"You're an idiot," shouted another.

"He's starting to sound like Ben Carson," Dad whispered. "That is never a good sign for a human being. I think President Lincoln has unnerved him."

"When I look upon America," Senator Arrogandez continued, "I see many millions of people who are walking the land in darkness. For the moment they are enemies, but I long to embrace them. I see perverts and Sodomites—most of them Democrats—as well as progressives and liberals, many of them Sodomites."

"Go sodomize yourself, asshole," a man shouted.

Two tomatoes just barely missed the senator's head.

"Does he know he's on the Upper West Side?" I said to Dad. He laughed and shushed me.

"I want to welcome all of these people, temporarily blackened by sin—atheists, infidels, pedophiles, liberals—with the loving arms of Christ, with my arms, and I want them to know that they too can once again be regarded as actual Americans if they repent. Yes, repent, and vote for me. I want to give them all seats at my table, to enjoy the bounties of my feast.

"Of course, not all of the seats will actually be at my table, strictly speaking. Some will be out back. But there will be nourishment for everyone. I have nothing but love in my heart for the most benighted and perverted among us, and I will tell these base creatures about my boundless love every day."

"Senator Arrogandez, one of the distressing thoughts I hear uttered by you and most Republican candidates is that God smiles upon your views. You seem absolutely certain of this. But what do you think of the extraordinary pluralism of this nation, the fact that people worship in hundreds of different ways—or not at all?"

For reasons I still don't understand, the question elicited an outpouring of candor that did not serve the senator well.

"You asked about religious faith? One of the joys of religion is that it makes you feel superior to other people. That's part of its glory. And how can you feel that you're part of something important if everyone and his brother gets to be a part of it, too? If everyone got into Harvard, would Harvard be Harvard? No! It would be Pipkin Community College, and that would be horrible."

Four more tomatoes landed on the stage, perhaps tossed by Pipkin graduates.

"My son Bob went to Harvard College."

"So you understand. Had he gone to Pipkin, you would be weeping now, mark my words. It is by looking down upon others and excluding them that we are able to feel so close to our fellow congregants and truly experience love. If you do not hate, how can you love? Without exclusion there can be no proper inclusion. And, therefore, we are nothing if not inclusive, very, very inclusive. We are exquisitely inclusive because we know so well how to be exclusive.

"May I tell an old Jewish joke?"

"Is it as old as I am?" Linc said.

"It's old, but it may not be that old. Anyway, after years of searching, rescuers come upon a man stranded on a desert island in the Pacific Ocean, an island, I should add, that has not been affected by any rising tides. And they are surprised to find that the man has built two synagogues on the island, neither of which has experienced any flooding. 'Sir, you have a very nice dry island here. Please tell us, why did you build two synagogues?' they ask. 'Oh,' said the man, gesturing to the one on the left, 'that one—I would NEVER go there.'"

The big laugh he got seemed to unhinge him further.

"I am not Jewish, but I get the joke. You can't discuss inclusion without also recognizing how important exclusion is. In this documented case I just addressed, even a man living alone on an island labored mightily to build a large synagogue that he never planned to attend. Not attending was the whole point."

"Wait," Linc said, "I thought that was a joke."

"But we know that jokes often contain a kernel of truth. I am talking about the kernel here. Even with scant hope that a rabbi—not to mention two rabbis—would swim by and begin officiating, the man built a temple that he did not intend to use because he followed his heart. People need to belong, and, perhaps as deeply, people need to NOT belong.

"Last year I was walking in New York on a very cold December day, not a hint of warmth in the air, with my good friend Morris Goldstein. We passed a synagogue and Morris said, 'I wouldn't be caught dead in that *shul*.' Well, the joke was on Morris because, three weeks later, he was. May he rest in peace.

"An Arrogandez presidency would be faithful to Morris's unintelligible last words and recognize the importance of belonging. And of not belonging."

I looked directly at Linc and noticed that his normal poker face seemed distorted. It had assumed the "I can't believe anybody is going to vote for this guy" look I had seen so often in my home over the years. But Linc rallied for his closing statement and so, I guess, did

Senator Arrogandez. At least he closed without telling another Jewish joke.

The two combatants shook hands. Both seemed somewhat perplexed, perhaps for different reasons. A Beacon official mumbled an apology and handed the senator a twenty to cover dry cleaning.

Heading home in a taxi, Mom said, "What got into Fred Arrogandez, thinking his joke was actually an anecdote?"

"I think he saw the opportunity to tell a lie he hadn't told before and couldn't pass up the chance," Dad said.

"It must be some kind of Crockenstock Effect," Mom said.

"Truth serum in reverse," Dad said.

"Linc, did you expect Senator Arrogandez to do something like that at the end?"

"Henry, no one could have expected that. It is indeed a brave new world you have here."

It was my cue.

> "O brave new world,
> That has such people in't!"

"And, Henry, it may require more bravery than you think to cope with them," Linc said.

Chapter 12

THE SURPRISE DEBATE at the Beacon did not help the standing of Senator Arrogandez with the general electorate, although it seemed not to hurt him with registered Republicans. During TV appearances, most rival candidates attacked the debate for excluding them and suggested they would have mopped the floor with President Lincoln had they been there.

Crockenstock's response the next morning was forceful, if unusual, even in the world of 2016 politics. He contended that because he wasn't there, the "debate" was a hoax. "People, you heard it here first, there was no debate." Crockenstock's supporters took this denial as a sign of strength. "He's just like Galileo," one man said, "always standing up to those who refuse to see the truth."

Nora Blitzen said that in addition to being a climate change denier, Crockenstock had now emerged as a debate denier. "Were you there?" Crockenstock responded. "Were you there? No? I didn't think so. Folks, it never happened. It never happened."

When a reporter said, "But Mr. Crockenstock, there were three thousand eyewitnesses to the debate," he replied, "But 320 million

Americans were not eyewitnesses. Which side of the argument do you want to take? You do the math."

Crockenstock's debate denial was perhaps the most appalling example of one of the enduring themes of the 2016 campaign, that there were indeed two sides to every story. There was observed reality and, well, on the other side, something completely different.

Saturday was a normal workday for all of us. I did more climate research for Linc's Cooper Union speech. Linc worked on his book and wrote notes for his *60 Minutes* appearance. At 2:00, Mom would take him to the CBS studio.

And then it happened.

It was commonplace to hear liberals say that conservatives lived in a bubble, hearing only opinions that reinforced what they already believed. Well, our six days with Linc had created a somewhat similar kind of bubble. We all assumed his noble nature would prevail and make the nation a better place. And then our bubble popped.

Our two landlines and four cell phones all started ringing at once. Oh no, I wondered, has there been a terrorist attack? I instinctively ran to find Mom, Dad, and Livvie before I even began talking on my cell. They all looked horrified.

Before I could ask why, Josh told me the Parasites website had just posted a story saying Lincoln's reappearance was a fraud engineered by the Mason family.

"A what?" I said.

"A fraud."

"Oh, shit. And they base this on what? Did they test the DNA?"

"Well, they said the Obama administration is part of the fraud. And they said you told Marshall Wendell it was all a hoax. I assume you didn't say that."

I laughed. "No Josh, I didn't. I didn't. Let me read the story and I'll call you back. Thanks for telling me."

"Anything I can do?"

"No, but thanks."

I went to the Parasites site. As cynical as we were about certain aspects of the system, we never expected this. Under the huge headline "DISHONEST ABE," the site said that Linc's "return" was the biggest political scam in history, that the DNA evidence had been concocted, and that the "notorious Mason family, known far and wide for its perfidy" was only in this to make a buck. (Given that we aren't rich, I guess perfidy does not pay.) The two named sources in the piece were Marshall Wendell, my favorite hedge fund manager, and Steve Turley, the former NYU history teacher whom Dad had beaten out for tenure. So they'd relied on two sources who hated us and never given us a chance to comment.

In case you didn't know, Parasites routinely promised sources and documents to back up its stories, but then, as if they had entrusted the paperwork to Nora Blitzen, the source material seemed to vanish. For reasons no human could adequately explain, the site remained fairly popular even though 80 percent of its stories turned out to be false. If you wanted to find someone on the wrong side of the story about where President Obama was born, what religion he practiced, and what was happening to the planet's climate, this would be your site.

We were all angry, but Dad was livid. "I'm going to sue those bastards," he said. "I'm going to put them out of business."

"My God, when did we become notorious?" Livvie said. "It's almost kind of cool."

"We might actually be able to put them out of business," I said. And then I paused.

"How?" Mom said.

"I taped my call with Wendell. This will all be okay." I went to get the tape.

When I played it, everyone relaxed and smiled. We had the legal upper hand, obviously, but we were all amazed that a man worth $2 billion, a person with children and friends whose opinions he presumably valued, would lie so baldly. On a risk/reward scale, trying to knock the Mason family off its pedestal—extremely short, as pedestals go—while risking your good name and, by extension, much of your fortune, was absolute lunacy. But Wendell did it. And now he was going to pay.

"Why would he do it?" I said. "And why tell me about extorting a better grade for his son?"

"If you crave power too much, it makes you crazy," Dad said. "It wasn't enough for him to have it. He had to tell everyone he had it. He had to crow. Because of his financial success, he may have become desensitized to risk. Think of Crockenstock and the ridiculous lies he tells when he doesn't really have to. It makes him feel good. He gets to live on the edge and demonstrate that he has a special power over reality, like a kind of warped superhero.

"Never doubt the power of The Big Lie. Hitler used it repeatedly, as did Johnson to get us deeper into Vietnam. Nixon won the presidency in 1968 by promising he had a secret plan to end the Vietnam War. That was a lie. Dick Cheney told virtually nothing but lies about Iraq leading up to our invasion. He helped convince more than 70 percent of Americans that Saddam Hussein was involved in the 9/11 attacks. That was a lie. It is human nature to think that when a person emphatically says one thing over and over again that he must be telling the truth. History suggests this is often not so.

"Because you and I would never do something so egregious, we naturally assume no one else would either."

Dad called his friend Walt McCall, a partner at a mid-sized law firm. Mom called the Chicken. What was she thinking?

Naturally, she got him immediately. His main virtue—perhaps his only virtue—was 24/7 availability. Then she gathered us for her report. "He says we should keep quiet. 'Never apologize, never explain' was his advice."

"That's exactly what destroyed John Kerry," I said. "The Chicken is a complete moron. I know one sure thing about political fights: when truth is on your side, scream like hell. Attack and then attack some more. With an opponent who has already shown a willingness to use The Big Lie, show no mercy. The Chicken is crazy. Are you sure he didn't say we should stay just a little bit quiet, maybe mumble something inaudible? Fire him and say if he breathes a word of anything we've discussed I will personally disembowel him."

"Do you really know how to do that?" Livvie said. She almost sounded proud of me.

"No, but I think there's a how-to video on YouTube."

Mom then called the White House and *60 Minutes* to explain our side of the Parasites story. Dad recounted the call with the lawyer, who had finally called back. "He said the Lincoln Foundation should sue Parasites for $15 million and the hedge fund tool for $100 million. He said we should be willing to settle for half of the $100 million but we should hang tough on the $15 million because that could put Parasites out of business. The fact that they never contacted us will really hurt them in court. Any money, of course, would go to the Lincoln Foundation. He said it would be nice if we could get on TV to get the story out to minimize damage to Linc's credibility."

Again Mom hit the phones. Within minutes, she said we had a shot of getting on *Face the Nation*. She'd find out after she took Linc to *60 Minutes*. It was remarkable how efficient Mom could be when she didn't solicit help from the Chicken. Now it was time for her to take Linc to the taping.

Then Uncle Ronnie called. Ronnie was Dad's younger brother who lived in Cincinnati. We had spoken to him briefly right after the FBI confirmed Linc's identity. Uncle Ronnie's one question at that time was whether Linc wanted to file a wrongful death suit against the family of John Wilkes Booth. Ronnie, you see, was a lawyer, an ambulance chaser who wasn't sufficiently swift or sleazy to get enough cases. Whenever we spoke, on the phone or in person, he almost always wondered whether a recent minor setback in our lives—a mediocre meal at a highly-rated restaurant or a disappointing visit to the podiatrist—wasn't worthy of a lawsuit. He liked to hear bad news from us, not because he wished us harm—no, not at all—but just because the worse the news, the higher the odds that we might become clients.

So as soon he learned of the Parasites story, he called. First, he commiserated about how the fiasco could devastate the Mason brand, then he started firing off questions. Dad saw the queasy look on my face. I put my hand over the receiver and told him what was happening. He grabbed the phone.

Dad told Ronnie about the secret tape and how we felt we had to act immediately and engage a New York lawyer. "Oh, Ronnie, I'm so sorry," Dad said. "I know how much you wanted to help after seeing the Parasites piece. But President Lincoln will be here such a short time, we felt we couldn't hesitate for a second. If anything like this ever happens again, you'll be our first call."

Oh my, something like this might happen again? What was our home going to become, a hostel for the eminent dead?

Dad made family small talk, then told Ronnie he had to go do more research for Linc. "Poor Ronnie," Dad said after hanging up. He said this after every call.

"Ah, inbreeding," I said, "never a good idea."

"If there was, you might be affected too. On a different subject, President Lincoln has been asking me for material on religion the last few days, especially views on specific Bible passages, but he didn't tell me why. I'm a little nervous."

"Well," I said, "this could be very good or very bad."

"Well, that was well put," Dad said. "Not quite up to the level of Inspector Clouseau, who said, 'There is a time to laugh and a time not to laugh, and this is not one of them,' but still quite pithy."

"I do try," I said.

We caucused about what we would say on TV in the morning—if we were on TV. I know I should have been nervous, but I was too focused on doing more research for Linc and on worrying about what he would say to *60 Minutes*.

When Mom and Linc came back, she told us that *Face the Nation* was a go. Linc's news was more problematic.

"Well, now I've done it," he said.

"What have you done?" I said.

"I've gone and done it."

"Could you be just a tad more specific," Dad said.

"I told them it was time to treat the Bible like the Constitution and amend it."

"Well, you're right," Dad said, "you have gone and done it. This will either be very good or very bad."

"Well put, Dad," I said.

"Are you sassing me?"

"Yes."

"You know what I want instead of sass. What do I want in the classroom?"

"Respect and fear."

"Yes, respect and fear. And what do I want at home?"

"Respect and fear." I paused. "Good luck with that."

And we smiled.

Mom and Livvie were amused, but Linc was not. "Henry, remember what we talked about at Lincoln Center?"

"Yes."

"Well, I think I've made a mistake. I think I finally said something that could damage my reputation forever."

We did our best to cheer him up, but before we could, the doorman buzzed up to tell us that Mom's younger sisters, Emily and Linda, were in the lobby. We had forgotten they were coming. And on this night, of all nights, when we had been "exposed" as scam artists. Emily and Linda would never let us forget that.

Neither sister had a satisfying life. They didn't enjoy their work and had five divorces between them. Their envy of Mom was sometimes extreme—and that was before we added the Lincoln Bedroom to our home—and it kept us from seeing them very often, even though they lived in the city. Mom usually felt bad when she avoided them and bad when she saw them. Like Josh's psycho parents, they didn't seem to aim for the jugular, but that's where their fangs often wound up nonetheless.

They each gave Mom a hug and said, "I'm so sorry, I'm so sorry." Their faces looked as if there had been a death in the family. No, get me rewrite. A death in a family they liked.

Within a minute, it was possible to gauge exactly how they felt. They didn't actually believe we were the Madoffs of politics, but entertaining the thought for even a moment was so delightful they couldn't absolutely dismiss it.

Dad brought Linc in to meet them. "I love your work," said Emily, using a phrase I suspect Linc had never heard.

"Oh, where have you been all my life, *Mr. President*?" asked Linda flirtatiously, putting very slight quotation marks around the honorific, to show she knew we had suffered a little setback.

"Dead, I should think," he said.

"I'm taking President Lincoln to the White House tomorrow to meet the Obamas and all the living presidents," Mom said. She might as well have told them that she had just won the New York, New Jersey, and Connecticut lotteries on the same day, can you imagine that? Her good fortune did not thrill them.

"Oh, have you told the White House about the Parasites article?" said Aunt Emily, ever hopeful.

"Yes. President Obama's people know from vast experience that almost *everything* Parasites prints is a lie."

"*Almost* everything," said Aunt Linda, changing the emphasis somewhat.

"So what are you going to do about it?"

"Well, I talked to our lawyer today," Dad said, "and we're going to file a libel suit and a defamation suit. Henry and I are going on *Face the Nation* tomorrow to discuss it."

Oh no, that was like telling them we had just won the Pennsylvania and Massachusetts lotteries as well. As they moved toward the living room, they saw Livvie and relaxed a little. They could relate to Livvie, and only Livvie, in a recognizably human way. She and her aunts slid gently into a discussion of clothes and make-up. Dad took drink orders. Linc excused himself to go back to work.

We survived the visit, though, I confess, my mind was elsewhere—on Linc, on *Face the Nation*, and on Grandpa Sam, Dad's father, who had died two years earlier, leaving me with no living grandparents. I had really loved Grandpa Sam. Almost every time I saw him, he'd say, "Abe Lincoln was the last honest man in politics. We need to find someone like him again."

Grandpa Sam was happy his son had become a Lincoln scholar—he felt responsible, and I'm sure he was—but I wondered how he'd react to seeing President Lincoln with his son and grandson. He'd probably feel responsible for that, too. I laughed at the thought. Would seeing Lincoln have cured Grandpa's despair at what politics had become? Maybe. He might have said, "Well, at least America has a chance now. But will the country actually listen to Lincoln? I think the country may be so far gone that people say, 'Oh, he's just an old coot with a beard. Ignore him.'"

And what would he have said about my political fantasies? "Beware the ides of March."

My aunts returned to their unsatisfactory lives, and we got back to the Lincoln project. After a few hours of work, I went to bed worried about what kind of pickle Linc had gotten into and about my network TV debut. I couldn't fall asleep for a long time.

Chapter 13

I DREAMED I WAS one of many Israelites in a crowd at the base of a mountain. Moses came down with two large tablets, except Moses was Abe Lincoln, and the words of the commandments had been changed. The first commandment was to observe a strict cap-and-trade policy for carbon emissions. "It was a good Republican idea before the Republicans ran away from it shrieking in terror," said Lincoln. "It must be embraced, else the seas will cover their golf courses."

Another commandment identified the percentage of energy usage that should come from renewables, with specific targets for the years 2020, 2025, and 2030. The masses seemed confused. The next commandments admonished me to respect and fear my father and to go easy on all siblings, especially those named Livvie. Since I was the only one in the crowd who seemed to comprehend these words, the Israelites began treating me as a wise man, the interpreter of the commandments.

"I am just a guide," I said. "I am just a guide."

"So lead us, lead us."

I didn't know what to do.

"Moses will be gone in four days and we will need a new leader."

"But I'm only thirteen," I said.

Then I heard a whisper about Bono and Henry Kissinger and they began chanting, "Lead us, lead us, lead us."

"What about Aaron?" I said. "He's the brother of Moses, and isn't he, like, your vice president?"

"Aaron is a putz," they replied in unison.

The idea of being responsible for so many people terrified me, and I woke up in a sweat.

It was about 6:00, time for me to visit a real leader. I poked my head into Linc's room, but he didn't notice I was there. With his right hand on his chin and the index finger above his lips and touching his nose, he was so deep in concentration that he looked like a statue.

A half hour later I tried again. This time he said, "Come in, Henry, come in."

"Hi. I had a weird dream. I dreamed that you were Moses and you brought down commandments about cap-and-trade and renewable energy."

"I wonder what the Israelites said to that!"

"They were very confused. They wanted me to lead them after your departure. How do you know if you want to be a leader and whether you'll be any good at it?"

"You can't know at age thirteen. Fred Arrogandez found out he was going to be president when he was still in diapers, and look what it's done to him. Don't be in a rush to know the answers to your questions.

"But I can give you some advice. First, make sure your heart won't be broken by any compromises you have to make. I've learned a new phrase since I've been back. 'Politics is the art of the possible.' It is a wise saying. Second, make sure you can live with yourself if you have to settle for a position below the presidency. You don't have to be the man on top. Third, if you believe in a great cause and feel that you can help guide people to a beneficial resolution, that alone may impel you toward leadership. You and I agree that climate change is that issue right now. But you are thirteen. The burning issue may be different when you finish your schooling. I certainly hope it will be different.

"Finally, you have to know how ambitious you really are. I hope you are less ambitious than I was. I was desperate to make my mark in politics, and I'm not sure I would have made a happy senator. I don't wish such ambition on anyone, because achieving the presidency is so unlikely. Sometimes, when reading *Macbeth*, I would talk back to the play, telling Macbeth to ignore the witches, ignore his wife, and be content with his new title of Thane of Cawdor. Of course, it is strange to give advice to a character in a play that you would have trouble taking yourself. I like to think I wouldn't have killed for the presidency. Anyway, the Constitution made it inconceivable. Part of the beauty of the American system is that, if you're not part of the government—and I was not—you can't kill your way to the top."

"They should add that quotation to the Lincoln Memorial! Which you are going to see today, I believe."

"So your mother has promised."

Mom yelled that Linc should be ready to leave for the airport in fifteen minutes. Part of me wanted to go with them, but Dad and I had to appear on *Face the Nation* from the CBS studio in New York. Afterward, I had to do research for Linc's Cooper Union speech and for letters he'd be writing to twenty-five billionaires. (That project would bring in $100 million. Nice work, Livvie.). Also, I decided that shaking hands with all the presidents and then being kicked to the curb, as it were, wasn't something I longed to do. I wanted to be in the room, of course. The White House had other ideas.

I thought about "The Room Where It Happens," Aaron Burr's great song about access and power in the musical *Hamilton*. At a dinner meeting, Hamilton, Jefferson, and Madison agree on a new financial system for the country, as long as the nation's capital is moved from New York to the Potomac. Just three men make these momentous decisions and Burr couldn't stand the fact that he wasn't there.

Today, the six presidents wouldn't be moving the nation's capital or changing our financial system, but they would be making some history. It would have been nice to have been in the room where that happened.

I decided to content myself by giving Linc information he might not have known. "George H. W. Bush's wife, Barbara, is a direct descendant of President Franklin Pierce," I said.

"Oh, he was a terrible president, almost as bad as Buchanan."

"Well, just don't say that to her."

"So you think I can't handle myself at a social occasion in the White House? Do you think I'm new at this? Do you know no history, young man?"

"You might be a little rusty."

"Any other tips you want to give me, a backwoods lawyer who became president after just one term in Congress?"

"Avoid dancing."

"But what if Barbara Bush asks me to dance?"

"Talk about President Pierce instead."

I said good-bye and went to go prep with Dad for our first national TV appearance.

Feeling about as ready as we were ever going to feel, and armed with the tape, we set off for the CBS studio on west Fifty-Seventh Street, on the other side of the island. John Dickerson, the host, would be interviewing us from Washington. First we talked about Linc the houseguest, then about Linc the political thinker. Then one of the people in the New York studio played part of the taped conversation with Marshall Wendell.

"And this is the man," Dickerson said, "who was one of the two named sources relied on by Parasites?"

"Yes," said Dad, "and the other source is a former colleague of mine in the History Department of NYU. I got tenure and he didn't.

I never realized how much this upset him until the Parasites article appeared. But back to Marshall Wendell. Besides the obvious lies he has told, I really questioned the man's stated values *before* he began lying about our family. The statements 'I'm a winner' and 'I always win' seem like prescriptions for unethical conduct, at worst, and shallowness, at best.

"Given the topic, I feel compelled to contrast Mr. Wendell's credo with that of Abraham Lincoln. President Lincoln was a tremendous success as a person and a president, but he did not always win. Far from it. He lost three elections—one for state legislator and two for senator—and one nomination fight for Congress. One of the things people love and admire him for is his resilience, his heroic perseverance despite enormous personal setbacks. And now, as perhaps the final insult this man has to bear, comes a wealthy hedge fund manager telling lies about my son and, by extension, about President Lincoln."

"Henry," Dickerson said, "people are going to wonder why you taped this call. Do you tape many of your calls?"

"Hardly any," I said. "But the day before I had an unnerving call with Master Elmore Mastiff, the headmaster of my school. He tried to extort President Lincoln's appearance at school by threatening me. I told him there probably wouldn't be time and I certainly didn't enjoy being threatened. That call put me on alert. In a way, I had also been put on alert by Crockenstock's propensity to lie about anything at any time. Truth is having a brutal season. So I put a tape recorder on my desk, just in case. I never foresaw this type of media attack, although I have long known about Parasites' hard-earned reputation for inaccuracy and sleaze."

Then Dickerson asked Dad if he had an announcement to make. "Yes, I do. The Lincoln Foundation for Improved Politics is filing a $15 million libel suit against Parasites and a $100 million defamation suit against Marshall Wendell. All net proceeds from the suits, if there are any, will go directly to the foundation."

Amazingly, within hours, portions of our appearance had gone viral and the linked phrases, "I'm a winner/I always win" had become a meme, a thing, in the modern meaning of that word. Millions of people clearly liked the idea of the "winner" being exposed as a ruthless fraud. I would like to think people who heard about this Wendell "thing" were less likely to divide the world into winners and losers, makers and takers. That would certainly be a good thing.

Someone even posted a song immortalizing Wendell's world view. A snippet:

> "I'm a winner
> I'll cut you down to size.
> If I can't do it cleanly
> I'll do it with lies."

As we headed home, we were bombarded by congratulatory calls. Livvie, who was working on Linc's social media strategy, texted that I spoke well and looked as if I belonged in this century. As for the downfall of our enemies, she said, "Yay! I can't wait." Wow. Considering the source, double wow! I particularly enjoyed a text from Josh. "Hey, Henry, you really smoked 'em! You sure put Master Mastiff in his place. As for Wendell, the stocks his fund owns are going to get creamed tomorrow as investors try to beat the rush out the door."

I'm embarrassed to say I had only considered how the Wendell tape would affect the Mason/Linc family business rather than the vast Wendell empire. Now that his character was revealed in all its despicable dreadfulness, at least some investors would decide his funds were too risky to be in. Aware that major withdrawals from Wendell's funds were inevitable, traders would sell shares in his biggest holdings now, in advance of redemptions.

How would Wendell respond? He could try the Crockenstock approach and deny ever saying what was on the tape, but, unlike Crockenstock, he didn't have millions of supporters who felt he couldn't possibly tell a lie sufficiently preposterous to offend them.

On the contrary, Wendell belonged to one of the most loathed classes on the planet. He was a hedge fund manager. People *wanted* to believe the worst about him. He was preloathed. In an information vacuum, most already hated him. Provide them with real ammunition and then, well, who knows?

Dad agreed that Wendell's lies would hurt him immediately, and he also said one surprise benefit of Linc's return might be the advent of more ethical behavior by leaders of Forbish Milton. "I'll believe that when I see it," I said. "I can only imagine how I'll be treated after attacking Mastiff and Wendell on national TV. Before, I thought this would be my last year at the school. Now it may be my last week or last day."

"We'll work it out," Dad said. "It's so stupid. The school could have had tremendous positive coverage from Linc's return, and now they've gone and turned it into a travesty. There's a lesson in that somewhere."

Back home, we watched a little of the White House festivities on TV. We saw Mom, who looked great, and Linc, who appeared exhausted, as if he'd just come from a vacation stay at Gitmo. "Maybe he needs sleep after all," I said.

"In a few days he'll get all the sleep he needs," Dad said. "Meanwhile, he has a lot of work left."

So Dad and I hunkered down, printing out and highlighting parts of articles and speeches to help with Linc's book and the Cooper Union speech. Oh, and then there was that billionaire letter project. Characteristically, Linc wanted to know as much as possible about each billionaire. "Oh, that one is a rich asshole" was not going to cut it.

I particularly enjoyed researching four tech billionaires who had purchased letters. Linc had actually talked to all of them—Elon Musk of Tesla and SpaceX, Jeff Bezos of Amazon and Blue Origin, and Sergei Brin and Larry Page of Google, which has funded the Google Lunar XPrize. (I must say that Googling the founders of Google was a kind of weird metasearch experience I had never had before. Very meta.) Linc and I were both fascinated, and unnerved, by the thought that these four geniuses thought it important to explore space travel so humans might be able to colonize other planets if we were ever forced to leave Earth. The contrast between how these megabrains viewed space travel—as a potential necessity—and how most of the idiots seeking the presidency regarded climate change—as a nonissue—was astonishing.

I was so engaged I lost track of time. Before I knew it, Mom and Linc walked through the door.

"How was it?" I said. "Did either of you insult Franklin Pierce?"

"It was great," Mom said. "It was a thrill to shake hands with all the presidents, even though I was shown the door immediately after my final handshake. But we knew that would happen."

"I did mention Franklin Pierce to Mrs. Bush," Linc said, "but I said nothing bad about him. Do you assume I'm just a rube with no manners?"

"Not at all," I said, "although I do like teasing you."

"One of the most interesting sites for me was the Washington Monument," Linc said. "When I was president it was only 154 feet tall and unfinished. Now it's 550 feet high and it looks great. I had a good time with all the presidents. They had many questions and were very deferential. I liked these presidents more than those we had in my day."

"Understandably," Dad said. "Historians believe the weakest group of presidents in a cluster occurred between John Tyler and you. Tyler, Taylor, Fillmore, Pierce, and Buchanan do not get much respect from historians."

"How was the Lincoln Memorial?" I said.

"As I told your Mom, it's hard to find the right words. I felt pride and gratitude, but I also felt some mistake must have been made for me to be honored in such a way. It is strange to find yourself memorialized. I felt more normal when I glanced at the words of the

Gettysburg Address and my Second Inaugural. I wrote those words. I spoke them. So it made sense to see them there. And Martin Luther King Jr.'s 'I Have a Dream' speech is also written on the memorial. I found it quite good and wonderfully moving."

After chatting a bit more, Linc took me aside. "Your mother is a very bright and lively woman. Quite lively."

"You see what I have to put up with? Did she give you a to-do list?"

"Indeed she did. And she told me all about the presidents I was going to meet. They should make more women like her."

"Oh, so you had the Starbucks reaction to her?"

"If you must put it that way, yes."

After dinner, we sat down in the family room to watch *60 Minutes*. Interestingly, Linc had been interviewed by Charlie Rose, a native of North Carolina, the eleventh state to secede from the Union.

"Oh, good Lord," Linc said, "do I really look like that?"

"TV is known for making you look ten pounds heavier and 150 years older," I said.

"Henry, I'm not joking," Linc said.

"No, you look much better than that," Mom said, asserting her role as the family diplomat.

"Thank you, Debra."

"You're here for just thirteen days?" Charlie Rose said.

"Yes, I'm facing very strict term limits," Linc replied.

"Why do you think that labeling candidates as liars when they're speaking on TV will work?"

"For two reasons. Yes, we want to change the behavior of some candidates and officeholders, but we also want to reduce voter cynicism, especially among young people. I hope that will happen, because many public servants and would-be public servants won't have the label affixed to them. Some politicians actually spend little or no time lying. Wouldn't it be refreshing to watch a debate between two people who were both telling the truth? Of course, they would still have some political differences, but that is how our system is supposed to work.

"My sense is that historians look favorably upon the debates I had with Stephen Douglas because, instead of lying about each other's positions, we used our time to articulate our views on the most important issue of the day, the expansion of slavery."

Linc then discussed his ideas for political reform at length. And then he said, "Let me just add one odd piece of history here that some viewers may not know. The woman I married, Mary Todd, was also courted by Stephen Douglas. So, to use a word I just learned, she 'dated' both the Republican and the Democratic candidates in the 1860 presidential election. I do not think any person in American history has ever been on such intimate terms with two opposing candidates for the presidency."

"I guess she really wanted to be First Lady," said Rose.

"Indeed she did, but my prospects for the presidency were fairly dim when she married me," Linc said.

"With each passing day, Ronald Crockenstock's attacks on you have grown more vitriolic and more personal," Rose said. "Listen to this."

They rolled tape and Crockenstock's voice rang out. "So this big loser, this lug-head who couldn't figure out what to do about slavery without starting a war that claimed the lives of almost 3 percent of the American people—that would be almost eight million people if the war had taken place today, just think about that—this overrated, ugly failure has the gall to come back and try to redeem himself at the expense of people, such as myself, who have really great plans for this country. This is an outrage. He should have remained dead, buried, and forgotten."

Rose's voice could be heard now. "Abraham Lincoln is hardly forgotten."

"Well, he should be. It would be good if he would be. And if he hadn't been shot—and he's so obnoxious it's pretty clear why someone would want to shoot him—then he would have been even more forgotten. Historically speaking, he had a good exit strategy. Martyrdom saved him from being seen by all as the failure he actually was."

"Are you suggesting that he should have been assassinated in 1865?"

"Absolutely not. I never said that. I never intimated that. I never implied that. But I stand by it."

"What do you stand by?"

"It."

"What is it?"

"It is it. As John Lennon said, 'Love is real, real is love.' And when I campaign, I feel the love."

The tape stopped and Rose looked at Linc. "Mr. President, would you respond to what Mr. Crockenstock said?"

"Truly, one does not know where to begin. I regret that I will presumably not be around long enough to hear Mr. Crockenstock state that the sky is green and the grass blue, although I sense that day is coming. The man is a sworn enemy of truth and decency. He is a menace to the American ideal."

"What do you think of his comments about assassination?"

"Again, he reveals himself to be something of an iconoclast. Most people are against assassination. I, certainly, am among them. But Mr. Crockenstock seems to be for it. He is a man of bold vision, like William Walker, the American adventurer who became president of Nicaragua, before being executed. I think Mr. Crockenstock might be well served by seeking the presidency of Nicaragua instead of that of the United States. Certainly, Americans would be."

"Are you suggesting that he be executed as Walker was?"

"As Mr. Crockenstock has falsely said so many times, I would like to truly say, 'I never said that.'"

"You said there are some things you want to say about religion. Please go ahead."

Uh oh, this must be where Linc thought he had really stepped in it. I glanced at him and he looked nervous. My stomach churned.

"Recently, I read an Internet comment by a woman who lamented that her children were being taught that many of the founding fathers were Deists. A Deist is a person who believes that God created the earth but is not involved in its day-to-day operations. He does not, for example, respond to prayer.

"This woman was upset that her children were learning that most of the founders did not have a personal relationship with Jesus Christ. Well, as it happens, most did not. Some weren't even sure if they believed or not. But the woman wanted to change the history of our country so that it better conformed to her religious views.

"It was not enough for her that Washington, Adams, Jefferson, Franklin, and others did great things. They had to have done these great things while believing as she did. But Adams, Jefferson, and Franklin, among others, did not. This is precisely where I begin to have a problem with how religion is taught to our young people. When you try to teach people about morality and start by lying, by distorting history, do you have any right—any reason—to expect a good outcome?

"Some of the religiosity I see in America today disturbs me, and I see it as a divisive force. The religious right feels that its freedoms are being abused, but I think this view is misguided. If anything, it is the religious right that is trying to impose its minority views on the rest of the nation. When I hear someone use the phrase 'Christian nation,' I wince. America is not a Christian nation and was never intended to be. A majority of its citizens happen to be Christian, which is fine and it may be ever thus, but that doesn't give Christians special rights to dictate policy for the millions of other Americans. America was meant to be a haven for people of all faiths, and for non-believers as well.

"I was surprised to read recently that President George H. W. Bush, whom I will meet the day this broadcast airs, once said atheists should not be viewed as citizens of the United States. I suspect he said this at a weak moment, without fully thinking through the implications, but this view clearly stands in opposition to the First Amendment and everything the founders stood for. Obviously, nonbelievers are allowed to be citizens. They are allowed to become president. There is no debate on this point.

"But I sense the former president is not alone in his view. When I see some politicians and opinion writers discuss 'the real America,' it is clear to me that they are discussing a group of people who practice Christianity much as they do and who read the Bible in a certain way.

"I believe that some of the most religious people in the country have some bad ideas, ideas that usually flow from a literal reading of the Bible. So I would like to propose what might look like a radical solution to many watching this program but to me only seems like common sense.

"The U.S. Constitution is a wonderful document, but the American people have seen fit to amend it twenty-seven times. All in all, it was good that they did so. It is my view that the Bible, a book I read almost every day of my adult life, needs to be amended as well. We might begin by removing those passages that are hateful, immoral, and illegal.

"Before you wail, curse me, and cover your ears, please try to consider this in an adult manner. I believe in God. I guess, given my present circumstances, it would sound strange if I said I *didn't*. But I only believe in parts of the Bible, and I think some portions are harmful for humanity. They were either always bad or are views that, as human knowledge has advanced, we've discovered are injurious.

"For example, the Bible commands us to kill our children if they curse us. It says we should stone people to death for heresy, adultery, homosexuality, working on the Sabbath, worshipping graven images, and practicing sorcery. The Bible also counsels that it is fine to sell your daughter into sexual slavery. In fact, the Bible says that slavery in all forms is perfectly acceptable and slaves should obey their masters, even harsh ones. The New Testament also praises another kind of subjugation, stating that wives should be subservient to their husbands. This did not happen in my marriage, by the way –even when I was president of the United States and, presumably, had significant power at my disposal—and I suspect there are many modern marriages in which it does not occur.

"I want to make two critical points. The first is that most rational people agree with me that these passages are wrong and sometimes cause great harm to innocent people. The second is that most people who claim to believe every word of the Bible actually do not. They may strongly oppose homosexuality and fight to limit the rights of homosexuals, but they don't even flinch when they see someone working on the Sabbath, nor do they think anyone should be killed for committing adultery. They would certainly not put to death a son or daughter who cursed them.

"Regarding the Bible this way borders on hypocrisy. Employing what some today call a 'cafeteria' approach to the Bible—in which you take what you want and leave the rest—can have pernicious consequences. I have been here only a week, but I have already heard so many people say that homosexuality is a sin and that the Supreme Court decision sanctioning same-sex marriage is wrong and must be overturned, and these same people have championed Kim Davis, the county clerk in Kentucky, the state in which I was born, who refused to grant marriage licenses to same-sex couples.

"Ultimately, all of these people would say that they know homosexuality is a sin. How do they know this? Because that is what God says. And where does He say it? In the Bible, of course. In both the Old Testament and the New Testament, as it turns out.

"Back in the nineteenth century, we used to joke about homosexuality. We knew very little about it. We certainly didn't know then what science knows today, that a considerable percentage of humans—there is some debate about the number—are born homosexual or become homosexual through a combination of biological and environmental factors. In any case, it is not their choice. And if it is not their choice, I don't see how it can be a sin. As the Bible reminds us, 'Judge not, that ye not be judged. For with what judgment ye judge, ye shall be judged.'

"I understand that thousands and thousands of lives have been blighted because homosexuals were not allowed to live as God made them. Many of these blighted lives ended in suicide. Some ended less dramatically, in simple despair.

"We do not have to conclude that God made a mistake in condemning homosexuality or that the men who wrote down what they believed to be God's word made a mistake. Now that the Supreme Court, and most of American society, has blessed same-sex marriages, I think it time that the passages in the Bible that treat homosexuality as a perversion and a sin—and even a sin punishable by death—should be excised. No book can be called 'good' that has such horrors in it. I also happen to think that when believers are taught they are superior to homosexuals, it also becomes easier for them to feel superior to other people who are different in some way."

I think he means you, Arrogandez, I thought.

"Many of you will think what I just uttered is a terrible, even evil, idea, and that is understandable. You have spent all of your lives believing otherwise. But I have yet to find anyone who could explain to me why it makes sense to condemn homosexuality, as the Bible does, but it does not make sense to follow ANY of the other Bible teachings I mentioned a few minutes ago.

"If you practice a cafeteria-style approach to the Bible, who gets to decide what goes on your plate? Your minister? Your priest? Your congressman? Your parents?

"I think it is important—even essential—for all of us to focus on those parts of the Bible that we reject on moral or legal grounds. I believe that if some of the misguided and hateful parts of the Bible were removed, you might actually see an increase in religious observance in this country.

"I feel in the twenty-first century as I felt in the nineteenth, that the Bible is the source of many of the problems that divide Americans. Mind you, I would have been a very different, lesser individual had I never read the Bible. But I think there are ways to improve it by removing a small number of portions.

"It is important to remember that the Bible has no legal standing in America. That is a good thing. Now, Senator Arrogandez says that the rules of God are higher than the laws of man, but, under our constitutional system, this is incorrect. But I do sympathize with his position. When I read the Supreme Court's Dred Scott decision in 1857, I knew it was wrong, both legally and morally. If you think that a legal position taken by a president, legislature, or high court is mistaken, you have the right to speak out against it or work to change it. You even have the right to ignore the law—as long as you are willing to bear the legal consequences, which can be quite severe if you stone your neighbor to death for working on the Sabbath."

"Were you a good Christian?" Rose asked.

"Oh, you have struck a nerve. That is a very difficult question. I tried to be so in my daily life and in my political life. But, as you know, I never joined a church. The people who accused me of being a Deist rather than a devout Christian were partly right. I remained confused on this issue until the day of my death."

"Has coming back to Earth, as it were, changed your view in any way?"

"I don't know yet. Ask me again right before I have to leave. When I was alive from 1809 to 1865, I certainly felt that there was a reason, something beyond me, that I was here.

"Lest anyone miss the larger point here, I want to say that I have heard about very few religious people who advocate killing those who work on the Sabbath or those who curse their parents or even those who lie with a person of the same sex, as sinful as they may see that conduct as being. And it's a good thing that they ignore such blood-thirsty biblical urgings, because all of them are illegal in our country."

"Did you think this way in the nineteenth century?"

"I did, but I chose not to speak out, because that would have destroyed any chance of having the political career I wanted. And when I was elected president, I thought someone would shoot me if I said such things. Once the Civil War began, I saw no point in saying something so controversial and potentially distracting when there was such urgent work to be done."

"Yet you feel free to say it now."

"In my case, death is a great liberator. I think this needs saying by someone people respect. In my case, it is an advantage that I will only be among you for a few more days. And I have no political ambitions or hopes for reelection. But now I see the seeds of a different kind of civil war being planted in these United States. I see people wielding the Bible as a weapon against gays, atheists, skeptics, Muslims, or those who simply read the Bible a little differently than they do.

"Those who consider homosexuality an 'abomination,' another word from the Bible, do not, as a rule, punish practitioners with death. Sometimes they do, but not as a rule, and when they do and are brought to trial, they receive little mercy if they are convicted. On this subject, the Bible should be amended.

"Today, slavery is rare in the United States. It is illegal and is viewed by virtually everyone as being immoral. So what is the value of keeping Bible passages that say it is a good and proper thing? Who benefits from that? On this subject, the Bible should be amended.

"I understand that to some of you this will seem like utter blasphemy. Who am I to be amending the Bible? Do I think I am God?

"One of my esteemed predecessors, Thomas Jefferson, amended his own Bible. He removed all the miracles. I am not suggesting that be done, but I find it interesting that the nation continues to revere Thomas Jefferson nonetheless.

"I would like to see a gentler view of religion in this great country, one that recognizes that the First Amendment gives us the right to worship as we please—or to not worship at all if that is what we please—as long as we don't violate any statutes as we do so.

"The beautiful words of the Bible—such as 'Love thy neighbor as thyself'—far, far outweigh the passages that bring hurt and shame to people unnecessarily. I also particularly like these words in Proverbs: 'A good name is more desirable than great riches; to be esteemed is better than silver or gold.' I wonder if Mr. Crockenstock is familiar with such thoughts.

"And yet. In my speech in this city, at Cooper Union, 155 years ago, I spoke of the importance of the founding fathers' views on slavery, but I cautioned against blind allegiance to precedent, saying that 'would be to discard all the lights of current experience—to reject all progress—all improvement.' Some of the words in the Bible deserve no such blind allegiance, certainly not the ones that reflect ancient biases against women and homosexuals and for slavery and the death penalty for the mildest of offenses—and sometimes for acts that really aren't offenses at all."

I turned away from the TV. Linc's face looked like a death mask. Mom, Dad, and Livvie looked stunned. I didn't know what to think, except that those who said Social Security was the "third rail" of politics didn't know what they were talking about.

Rose, ever the professional, paused before sympathetically saying, "You know some people are going to hate what you've just said?"

"That is a certainty. I don't want there to be less religion in America. I just want some of what passes for religion to be less punitive. We need more tolerance, especially by people of faith who believe those without that faith are wrong and even damned.

"Presidential candidate Marco Rubio has said that 'God's rules always win,' which is a terrifying, baseless, and lawless formulation. This view is un-American. I know he says this, in part, to court the religious right, but such foolish statements can have broad impact. It can affect how children are taught. On that note, I think Americans have to stop demanding that religion triumph over science in the schools when the two worlds conflict. Teaching children things that are untrue, whether about the religious beliefs of the founders, the age of the earth, evolution, or climate change, is bad for the nation. Science and religion can coexist. They have to. And when they conflict, the nation's leaders must allow science, and not religion, to determine policy. If you allow religion to make these decisions, you have created a theocracy, something antithetical to what the founders intended."

"But who would be in charge of amending the Bible?"

"I don't have a wonderful answer. If it happens at all, I would assume that it would start with a few congregations whose leaders and parishioners thought it a good idea. Then it might spread slowly. There won't be a commission that does this. How will other countries respond? I don't know. Clearly, I understand that, right now, the vast majority of people who have worshiped the Bible will not want to change it. But some of their children or grandchildren may feel differently one day. My goal here is simple: I want religion to be more tolerant and more compassionate, and I want fewer people to be hurt by religious teachings. This is a problem that extends way beyond the King James Bible, but that is the book I am addressing right now."

"Do you think you were given a second chance at life so you could speak these words?"

"Possibly. My friend Henry thinks so, but I can't say any more because I simply don't know. But I do want to add a few words about Henry, a very special thirteen-year-old boy I met a week ago. Henry Mason has proved a most excellent guide to the twenty-first century. He is intelligent, learned, decent, and very funny. I also suspect he is incorruptible. Now, Henry may want to guide some of you one day, and that could be a good thing. If some of the political improvements we have discussed tonight occur, Henry might consider a career in politics. Given that possibility, I made him a campaign poster. It says, 'Henry Mason is a good man who deserves your vote. A. Lincoln.' If, in the future, Henry has the desire to use this poster, I just want you to know that it is genuine, as is my high regard for him."

Well, there it was, the ultimate life-in-a-trance moment. My family just stared at me. Linc smiled. Sure, only he had known what was coming. Of all the thirteen-year-olds in all the world, Abraham Lincoln had touted me on TV as a future leader, with a campaign poster to boot. "Thank you, Linc," I said. "Thank you." I felt good, then numb, then overwhelmed. I ran to my room. I closed the door and started crying.

After a few minutes, Mom knocked and I let her in. She gave me a brief hug. "What's the matter?"

"Did anything ever happen to you that was too good, that was so far beyond your expectations that you didn't know how to handle it? Everything with Linc has been beyond amazing, and now he does this. I'm very happy and a little scared that the highlight of my life probably just happened. I fear I may have peaked too soon."

"We've had an experience no other family has ever had. That doesn't mean the rest of your life is going to be a letdown. But it is going to be different. And it's certainly going to be different when President Lincoln leaves. I bet that's part of what might be making you a little sad."

"I've felt so motivated and useful since he arrived. It's how I want to feel for the rest of my life."

"That's wonderful. And you can feel that way a lot of the time, even without a beloved dead president staying in your home. After this week, I'm more convinced than ever that you will find something that engages you thoroughly. Your father has."

"And you?"

"I like my job well enough, but it's not a calling. But lots of people hate their jobs. They can't wait to get home to watch TV or go to the mall to buy something they don't really need or can't afford so at least they'll have something to show for tolerating their awful job. So I'm not worried about you, but I am a little worried about Livvie."

"Linc has brought out the best in her. Well, no matter what happens, couldn't she always work for the Kardashians in some capacity?"

"Perhaps. But does that sound like a satisfying life's work?"

"Not to me."

"Nor me. You know, you probably think Livvie fits into her world better than you fit into yours."

"She's always FaceTiming someone. She's in constant contact with her squad."

"But the people who achieve something special often don't fit in so well at first. Look how lonely President Lincoln was when he was young. Fitting in may be what Livvie does best. That can be fine for junior high and high school, but afterwards it's not a talent that necessarily gets you very far."

"Couldn't she manage some celebrity's social media presence?"

"Perhaps. But what about a life beyond social media? She's not exactly bookish."

"No, she's textish. But she's popular and I'm not."

"When you're older you'll see that the quality of your friends is more important than the quantity. And after President Lincoln's visit, your quantity may change too."

"I'll try to exploit my fame, such as it is, only a bit. But will Josh still prefer Ethan to me?"

"Would you want him to change because you know Lincoln?"

"Yes."

"Really?"

"Well, maybe. Why do we want people to care exactly as much about us as we care about them?"

"Because we are all insecure and easily hurt."

"You?"

"Oh, adults are just better at hiding it. We've had lots of practice. So, are you ready to rejoin the group and see if they're coming with pitchforks for your friend the Bible amender?"

"Sure, after we check to see if any political parties are launching a Draft Henry movement."

"Henry!"

"I'm kidding. Just a little fame-based humor."

As I entered the room, I got a call from Josh. "May I speak to the anointed one?" he said. "And may I come over to touch the hem of your garment?"

"I'm sorry, hem-touching is only available on weekdays from 5:00 to 6:00 p.m. We're closed right now. Ahem. Josh, this is really weird, being anointed and all."

"Face it, you're President Lincoln's boy toy."

"Hey. Watch it. I'm his friend and guide."

"And he's your campaign manager and will be forever, even from the grave."

"Wait, you know I'm not running for anything unless the process gets cleaned up. So what did you think about his Bible idea? He never told us that was coming."

"I think it's great. But I'm a cynical son of a bitch. Removing any part of the Bible is fine with me, especially the stuff about Jews and Christians."

"That would take care of the whole Bible."

"Oh, right."

"Moving right along, do you think people at school are going to hate me because of what Linc said?"

"Linc?"

"Oh, that's what he likes me to call him."

"You're in pretty deep, aren't you?"

"I know, I know. But back to the hatred question."

"Most won't. They'll think it's cool. People are suckers for fame. And some of the assholes will try to cozy up to you now in hopes that down the road you might be able to do favors for them."

"Okay, I think I can handle that. Question: If I let them suck up and do shit for me, do I have to do them the favors later or can I blow them off? I need a ruling."

"You know, Henry, you may be the first thirteen-year-old who has ever asked that question. At least I hope you are."

"Sorry, I guess I was pushing it."

"You should know that my parents are on my case because of you. They're more afraid than ever that I won't amount to much, and they strongly suggest that I exploit my relationship with you to get a job."

"Well, Josh, the transition team's first meeting isn't until next week. Man, your folks are setting new records for crazy."

"Tell me about it. Instead of being excited about Lincoln's mentioning you, my father pointed at Lincoln and said, 'Schmuck, what about Josh? What about Josh?' I think he saw it as my last best hope for a decent career. Then he threw things at the TV."

"What did he throw?"

"Chips and guacamole. Together and separately. Like you, he always wanted to be a pitcher. I hope you won't be as bitter as he is if you don't make it."

"I think you need to impose some severe eating restrictions on the man. Anyway, tell your dad that as president I will establish the office of consigliere and that you're my first choice. Now I have to go see what the rest of the country thinks about Linc's idea."

"My advice is don't forget to duck."

I went back to the family room and the TV. To no one's surprise, the religious right jumped all over Linc's Bible proposal.

"Who would be chosen to amend the Bible?" asked one irate minister. "Secular humanists? Democrats? Satan himself?"

"We picked Satan for the job," Dad yelled at the TV, "because he came in with the low bid."

A former southern governor and minister said, "Sir, you may have led us once, but you are in great danger of leading us astray now. There is only one, sir, who has risen from the grave, and you are not He. Go on, be off with you. Get back from whence ye came!"

"What's with the 'Get back from whence ye came' stuff?" Mom said.

"Oh, he probably just had four Chick-fil-A sandwiches for dinner and I think they went straight to his head," I said.

A Texas televangelist who said that after the Supreme Court's decision on same-sex marriage "love affairs between men and shellfish will soon have legal standing" suspected that Linc wasn't really a messenger from God. "I have it on good authority that he has been sent not by God but by Satan," he told Fox News. "My source is a very high-level celestial authority, He who cannot be named. I gave Him my word that I would not disclose His identity. He is the ultimate Anonymous Source."

"Hey, Linc," I said, "did Satan send you? That would be a really lousy thing for you to do to this family."

"I don't think so, but if he did that was very devious of him. That would be very satanic. Even I would be impressed."

Some moderate religious figures actually said Linc had articulated something they had thought about for a long time. What was the value, they said, of having many passages in the Bible that were clearly relics of an earlier time and now defied current American laws as well as common sense?

"The Bible tells us that gays are sinners and that we should hate them and even kill them," said one minister. "But those are ancient thoughts that are no longer compatible with our laws or with most people's sense of decency. As far as I can see, no one benefits if we continue to preach such hate."

Still others thought Linc's words might be a message from the divine. Livvie was monitoring online developments, and she said many bloggers speculated that Linc might be God's messenger and that his words should be given special weight. "If you were God and realized you wanted to make changes to the Bible," one columnist wrote an hour after the show, "how would you do it? Would you have a guy named Stan, an assistant manager of a Burger King in Terre Haute, Indiana, step forward and announce that, after coming home from a night of bar-hopping, he lay down on the sofa and then God told him he'd like to make the following Bible edits? Or would you instead consider sending one of your most successful and beloved creations—Abraham Lincoln—back with your message?"

I found that a very interesting take on Linc's "revelation." For the first time in my life, I tried to put myself in God's shoes. (My arrogance quotient had, you might say, been stoked by recent events.) If you were the creator, how would you effect a biblical rethink? "Ah, Lincoln, good man, that Lincoln. And respected! A righteous man. Never lied. And a martyr." And if Linc were indeed an instrument of God's will, maybe some of his political reforms might actually occur.

But then I felt like screaming. I had always thought that Linc's purpose was to reform our political rather than our religious life. But now millions were probably going to hate him for being a false prophet. They were going to focus only on what he said about the Bible and not understand that his objections to parts of it were really political rather than religious. He was concerned about the civil rights of gay people and women. But would anyone really hear what he was saying?

Certainly, neither Crockenstock nor Arrogandez did. "Those things they showed me saying on *60 Minutes*, well, I never said them," Crockenstock began. "And I can prove it," he lied. "Now, this idea of amending the Bible is absolutely crazy, vicious, and egomaniacal. I have it on good authority that he intends to replace every mention of 'Abraham' in the Old Testament with 'Abraham Lincoln.' You just watch and see. This is a scriptural land grab such as the world has never seen."

"I wish I knew before our Beacon Theatre debate that he had this insane and offensive plan, but he was too cowardly to tell me," Senator Arrogandez said. "God made man in His image, but now Lincoln is trying to make God in his own image. He looks upon this beautiful Bible that has served mankind so well for two millennia, and he has a hissy fit and says like a four-year-old, 'I wanna change it, I wanna change it. It makes me feel bad, it makes me feel bad.' If we made these changes, God might be so angry that he would dispatch several asteroids to smash into Earth and kill four billion of our people, perhaps even some in my home state. And He would be right to do so.

That would be no more than we deserved for our effrontery. If there were an eleventh commandment, it would be 'Edit me not.'"

"This is why we need the Prediction Assessment score so badly," Linc said. "That is one of the most mindless predictions I have ever heard."

Needless to say, every TV talk and news show was completely devoted to Linc. We were channel-surfing like crazy. One firebrand preacher said, "I call for the earth to open and suck him up, for God to show his wrath by crushing his bones, burning his flesh, plucking out his eyes, and leaving nothing behind but a bloody beard."

"Oh, dear," said Linc. He then said he was going to work on his book. "I confess," he said, "that I feel like one of the witches in Macbeth, stirring the pot:

'Double, double toil and trouble
Fire burn, and cauldron bubble;
Cool it with a baboon's blood.
Then the charm is firm and good.'

Good night."

The rest of us continued to sit transfixed by the TV. "What I'm seeing reminds me of some business meetings I've been in," Mom said.

"The burnt flesh and eye-plucking part?" I said.

"No, not that. Well, okay, maybe a little. What I really meant was that some of the people seem to have feelings they're not expressing. They're nervous. They're afraid to be out front saying that a chunk of the Bible is absolutely awful by our current standards. Suppose their boss or their boss's boss disagrees? Why commit to that view on TV before you see what other people think? A lot of these people are doing a risk/reward analysis, and the risk for being wrong seems a lot greater than the reward for being right. That's why some of these talking heads, who are used to blathering comfortably about anything, including things they know nothing about, seem to look so uncomfortable tonight. Most have never discussed their religious beliefs publicly. They're walking on eggshells."

She was right. The shows had booked the secular talking heads before they knew what Linc would say. Now some of these aberrantly chatty folk had looks that reminded me of a little kid playing right field in a softball game and softly praying, "God, please God, don't let them hit the ball to me."

Chapter 14

ONE OF MY first thoughts when I woke was that there was a chance today would be more about politics than religion, and thank goodness for that.

Wrong.

I turned on the TV and learned that some members of the cloth, having had a chance to sleep on Linc's Biblical amendment idea, had decided that the best way to show Linc what they thought of it was to violate the sixth commandment and kill him. In addition to violent pronouncements from many pastors, some law enforcement officials reported that there might now be a bounty on Linc's head. Multiple teams of hit men, known as "God Squads," were apparently set to descend upon the city.

The FBI called at 7:00. Supervisory Special Agent David Butler told us the threats were real and that we should consider restricting Linc's public appearances. The bureau would station several agents in our building as a protective detail.

Linc was remarkably unperturbed. "Maybe it's the fact that I've already been assassinated or that I know my time is up soon anyway, but I'm not scared. Absolutely the worst thing the religious right could do for its cause would be to kill me for what I just said. I have already revealed a talent for martyrdom. The crime would look not only hateful but also profoundly stupid, given what you might call my expiration date."

"This is America," I said. "Hateful and stupid things happen all the time. Look at Crockenstock. He eats hateful and stupid for breakfast."

"Whatever that means, I suspect it is true," Linc said. "And, who knows, maybe I've been sent back precisely to get shot again. What kind of person must you be to get assassinated twice?"

"An inspiring one?" I said.

"Oh, but the things that I inspire," said Linc.

From TV we learned that Linc's *60 Minutes* appearance was the most watched event—by far—in the history of the planet, with almost 50 percent more viewers than any Super Bowl. Wow. More people who might get excited about his reform ideas. And more people who might want to kill him.

A half hour later, one of the morning shows had two lawyers debate what word to use if Linc were to be gunned down again. Would it be an "assassination?" Or a "reassassination?" Or a simple murder, since death in 1865 had deprived the late president of his presidential status? It is fair to say that they beat this particular horse to death. One lawyer added, unhelpfully, that "if the antizombie legislation being discussed in the House were signed into law and Abraham Lincoln were declared a zombie, then killing him wouldn't be a crime at all. It would be a lesser offense than jaywalking."

"Oh, that lawyer's mother must be so proud!" Dad said. "Maybe this will lead to the creation of twenty more 'God Squads' since some members could contend they were innocent no matter how vile their actions."

"Hateful and stupid marches on," I said. "The lawyer would probably accuse me of being rabidly prozombie because I'm trying to use all my energy to help Linc while he is here.

"So Linc, aren't you at least a little worried?"

"No. People who called me a fatalist were correct. I believe you have to work as hard as possible for what you believe but that the outcome is determined by powers greater than you. You said I had the option of going to a beach and playing shuffleboard, whatever that is. Having come this far, I see absolutely no appeal in the beach vacation option. There is a battle for the soul of America raging out there, and I want to be a part of it. It is my destiny to say what I believe and accept the consequences. It always was."

The doorbell rang. Mom went to the door and let in the atrocious Mrs. Maggert. "Do you know that there are men with guns downstairs? Your son brings in a bum from the homeless shelter and now there are fiends with guns downstairs! And there's another man with a gun sitting right outside your apartment."

I poked my head out. What a shock, she had told the truth.

"Mrs. Maggert," Mom said, "those men are FBI agents, and they are here to protect President Lincoln. Henry only told you that story about the shelter because we had not yet confirmed the president's identity. You have heard that President Lincoln has come back?"

"I heard some people say it but I didn't believe it and I still don't. If Lincoln came back, I doubt he would stay with slop heads such as yourselves. The man you have here still looks like a bum. Well, at least he's found a place where he fits in."

"Mrs. Maggert," Mom said, "do you always have to try to be the most awful person in the building? Are you trying to become the most awful person in all of Manhattan? You insult us all the time, and now you've even found a way to disrespect President Lincoln. I'm sick of it. In the future, please be so kind as not to utter any of your poisonous words to members of my family. If you say a single word that isn't decent or respectful, we will do everything in our power to see that you are kicked out of the building. And, by the way, my son, Henry, whom you treat so abysmally, is now a national hero for helping President Lincoln. So if you think we have no influence, just try us. Oh, and one last thing. The men with guns are on our side, so watch your step. Good day and goodbye, Mrs. Maggert."

Mrs. Maggert turned around and left, slamming the door behind her.

"Wow, Mom, what got into you?" I said. "What happened to 'live and let live'?"

"Oh, I don't know," she said, as we stood in the foyer. "President Lincoln is having his life threatened for speaking the truth, and I just felt the least I could do was finally talk back to her. Maybe no one ever does. Being a raving lunatic has its benefits. People are either too afraid to confront you or they think that the path of least resistance is just to avoid a showdown. But that's ceding a victory to her that she doesn't deserve."

"Sometimes a person's mother just tells him not to mind the crazies."

"And sometimes the mother realizes she is wrong. Mrs. Maggert is vicious but not dangerous. It's okay to swat her and try to make her back down. I don't want to dread seeing her in the elevator. I want her to dread us."

Then she paused. She looked as if she now realized exactly what she had done and was happy about it.

"Now, the people pursuing President Lincoln are both vicious and dangerous, a totally different story."

"Can we really get Mrs. Maggert kicked out of the building? That would be so great."

"Alas, no. It was an empty threat. But that didn't make it any less enjoyable to say."

"Mom, you're changing."

"You know, there's something about having Lincoln here. Part of it is seeing him have the courage to risk his impeccable brand." I gulped a bit. "But more things just seem possible since he's been around."

"Guys, come see this," Dad said from the living room. He had CNBC on, a rarity for him, and the topic was our favorite hedge fund manager. Joe Kernen, the makers-and-takers anchor who usually cravenly defended all rich people against attacks from the nonwealthy, had apparently finally seen a billionaire behave in a way that appalled even him.

"When you trash an entire family publicly and then a thirteen-year-old boy has the whole thing on tape, you're really up a creek without a paddle," Kernen said. "Wendell's fund is already having a subpar year, and it's about to get much worse today. Many of his favorite stocks are already down 5 to 10 percent in pre-market trading, which would cost his fund hundreds of millions of dollars. Short-sellers are salivating as they target these stocks. The line of people wanting to redeem some or all of their investment is already winding around the block."

The last flourish, Dad explained, was purely rhetorical. Redemptions could occur only at certain times of the year, with all transactions done by email or phone. Still, the run on the bank image appealed to me. At least something was destined to go right today.

On that note, I headed to school. Even though my folks understood that my stretch at Forbish Milton would soon be up, they thought it wise that I put in an appearance. Linc and some foundation directors would be holding a press conference partly based on work I had already done on how to get young people to become better informed and care more about politics. My help really wasn't needed.

I felt so many different kinds of strange all at once. It seemed as if my "real" life was back home helping Linc, so leaving that made me feel adrift. And going to school instead? After all that had happened, including my appearance on *Face the Nation* and the amazing things Linc had said about me last night on *60 Minutes*, there was no way that seeing my classmates and teachers and, oh please no, Master Mastiff, was going to seem normal. Finally, as I walked to school from the subway, Patti Smith's *People Have the Power* started playing in my head, and I savored one of my favorite lines about people being able "to redeem the work of fools." Oh, were we in need of redemption.

To me, it was a rock update of the conclusion of the Gettysburg Address. But it wasn't playing just as a rock anthem. It seemed like my personal theme song and suddenly I was like a character in a movie. That may sound cool, but when you've spent thirteen years struggling to feel like a human being, it's way more weird than cool. After all that had happened since I met Linc in Central Park, I really, really didn't need a fuckin' theme song to make me feel special, but I seemed to have one nonetheless.

I had texted Josh to meet me by the Starbucks a block from school. Seeing him brought me closer to normal. "Can we talk for a minute without using the word 'anointed'?" I said.

"Yes, my liege," he said.

I burst out laughing. Ah, sarcasm to the rescue. And boy did I need it. We started walking to school.

"Now, Josh, I'm going to be needing a wartime consigliere. Are you sure you can handle it?"

"Yes, but who are we fighting?"

"Oh, we have many enemies. But tell me, Josh Edelstein, that's a Jewish name, isn't it?"

"Sicilian on both sides. We changed it."

"Glad to hear it." Of course, at that moment, I saw Master Mastiff heading toward school and he saw me, which made us both supremely uncomfortable. Couldn't some teacher or student go up to him and start talking so he wouldn't focus on me? "Josh, quick, can I hide in your pants?"

"Gee, Henry, fame has messed with your brain. I have no room for you in my pants. I don't even have room for your sister in my pants, although in her case I would give it a try."

"Too late, anyway. Master Mastiff saw me."

"Relax," he said, as he opened the school door and we headed toward our lockers. "Sure, he hates you and wants to kill you. But he won't. You make him much more nervous than he makes you."

"Not possible."

"Oh, but it is, it is. Any school in the world would take you now. Even Brearley."

I laughed. It's an elite Manhattan girls' school.

"Master Mastiff isn't sure any school would want *him*." Another pronouncement from Josh, and, of course, he was right. I had the upper hand. Oh no, the Patti Smith song started pounding in my brain again. Talk about things going to your head.

"So how was your weekend?" I said, very happy to change the subject.

"Mom and Grandma got in all the fighting they needed. They went fifteen rounds. Lots of blood but no serious injuries. Dad and Grandpa played beer pong, but they had a beer whenever one of them missed the cup. That sped things up nicely. I mostly got ignored, thank goodness."

Josh and I headed to history and sat next to Gillian. She gave me this wonderful smile and a small thumbs-up sign. "The shows were great yesterday," she said. "How are you going to use your power today?"

"We all thought I should go to school and try to blend in with the little people."

"How is that working?"

"Too early to tell. Mastiff seemed horrified to see me."

"Good. Do you think he had Wendell lie about you?"

"Probably not. Wendell's money will always insulate him. As far as I know, Mastiff has no fortune to fall back on. I assume he needs a job."

Mr. Farmer silenced all of us. "It is so nice to see the return of our prodigal son, Mr. Mason. Welcome."

"It's nice to be here."

"Is it?"

"Well, some extraordinary circumstances have kept me busy."

"Do you want to become president, Mr. Mason?"

I paused. How should a thirteen-year-old handle that one in public?

"The world would like to know," Mr. Farmer said.

"Not if the system still stinks. And it stinks now. Before I say anything else, I want to apologize to you and the class for not bringing President Lincoln here. He needs to do so many things before he is taken from us that I didn't want to pile one more item onto his schedule. But, please, I will answer any questions you have."

"What have you learned about President Lincoln that we might not know?" asked Mr. Farmer.

"First, he's really nice. And he knows so much. He knows poetry and history and what drives people, and he knows all this despite having had just one year of formal schooling."

"Is that why you've been avoiding formal schooling of late, Mr. Mason?"

"No, Mr. Farmer. Living with President Lincoln has changed my life in many ways, but it hasn't changed my view of education. I've been absent because I was trying to help President Lincoln."

"Well, I regret not meeting him."

"And I regret not bringing him."

"Do you think his return will really change the world?" Mr. Farmer said.

"All along, I assumed it would. I just had this deep belief that a huge number of Americans wanted the political process to improve and become less pathological."

Mr. Farmer then asked the class what it made of Linc's return. Some thought the system would improve. Others were dubious. Some desperately needed caffeine or more IQ points or both.

Another group in need of more IQ points—the assholes—made their move at lunchtime. Clearly, the two Sunday TV shows led them to reassess my value in ways that the mere presence of Lincoln in my apartment had not. Now I had made the move from Nobody to Hip Important Person.

"So what's he really like?"

"What has he told you about politics?"

"Do you think you'll really be president someday?"

For the first time in my life, these people had lots and lots of questions. But the encounters were disorienting. When mild disdain turns to fawning fascination virtually overnight, you don't feel triumphant. Instead, you marvel that other people have this entirely new take on you, and it feels really bizarre because you're still trying to figure out how much you have actually changed.

"Sir, may I carry your backpack?" Josh said when school was over.

I smiled. "Josh, you were right as usual. The assholes were all over me today."

"I can see the headline in the *Post*: 'Young Man Covered with Assholes!'"

"A lovely image. But what am I do with such a profusion, such a confederacy of dunces?"

"Are you sure you're allowed to say 'confederacy' this week? Anyway, you'll figure it out. Just remember, they're voters."

"Yeah, if I could only stay at this place and get those votes. We have to talk about that. But for now, do you want to come back with me and we'll get the report on Linc's press conference today?"

We headed home.

Linc was in the living room talking to Livvie. Now, there's a meeting of the minds! Oops. Come on, Henry, think nice thoughts about your sister.

"Hello, Josh," Linc said. "I was just telling Olivia that we had a fine day today."

Linc then told us about the press conference, and as he did it hit me that he was the antithesis of Crockenstock, and not merely in his affection for truth. Linc never praised himself when he talked. In fact, he liberally gave credit to others, even for ideas that were actually his. We watched some of the taped press conference on C-SPAN.

The foundation board members who spoke at the midtown hotel ballroom said unequivocally that the country would benefit if we paid citizens to read selected articles about politics. The foundation could launch the paid reading program—nicknamed "Pay as You Grow" by one speaker, in a nice slap at you know who—in less than two months and would include a weekly lottery with $100,000 in prize money. To no one's surprise, a reporter asked if the program wasn't putting democracy up for sale.

"That's an interesting question to ask, following the Citizens United decision that allowed corporations and rich individuals to contribute limitless funds to candidates both directly and indirectly," Linc said. He stood up and walked around the front of the room as he spoke. "This program is not about buying votes. It is about using financial incentives to make the public better informed about crucial issues. Think of it as a kind of reverse taxation. And, in implementing it, we hope to diminish some of the extreme partisanship so prevalent today. This is truly an attempt to help people on opposing sides begin to understand how their fellow citizens think. I fear many Americans are losing the capacity to do that."

He paused, apparently hoping that people on both sides would let this idea sink in.

"Perhaps this will lessen the desire both sides have to 'take their country back' from the opponents who, they suspect, are out to ruin it. Despite what some of you may think, no one in elected office has set out to ruin the United States of America. Although, understandably, it sometimes seems that way.

"Just one other thought. We invite you, the public, to make donations to help the Lincoln Foundation improve democracy in America. Now, I understand if you are reluctant to contribute anything before you see how the program functions. You don't want to buy a pig in a poke. By the way, do you know the derivation of that expression?"

His face lit up a bit, as it so often did when he was about to tell a story. "People used to sell what they said was a suckling pig in a bag you were not allowed to open. Why anyone ever thought this a good way to encourage honest dealing is beyond me. When the buyer eventually opened the bag, he or she often found a cat or a dog, both of which amounted to an unhappy surprise, nutritionally speaking.

"We have no intention of sticking you with a dog or cat. But please, put a note in your calendars three months from today or six months from today to make a contribution if you think we are on the right track. I'd love to stop by to remind you, but I doubt that will be possible. And if you deem this effort unworthy in some way, instead of just gnashing your teeth, please contact the foundation and let those good people know how they can improve things. We want to make our democracy stronger. We want to hear your voice. After all, one of our many goals is to increase voter participation to a level close to what it used to be.

"I am spoiled on this score because back in the Stone Age, in the election of 1860, one of my favorite elections, 83 percent of all eligible voters voted. I believe you have a better transportation system than we had then. Please, for the sake of the country, avail yourselves of it in November of 2016. Thank you."

Then a flock of educators ranging from the elementary school level on up to graduate school spoke about how they intended to implement the paid reading program, as well as the political discussion groups, where they worked. Those spearheading the plan were bathed in the warm glow that can only accompany a bright new idea that has not yet been tested in the marketplace.

Not that I was cynical about the program. I wasn't. I just wanted to see proof that it could come anywhere near achieving its goals. I didn't want to find that the closed sack I'd dragged home contained a dead dog or cat. Yuck.

When we had finished watching highlights of the event, Mom came in and announced that Linc's Cooper Union speech had sold out. It would raise an additional $3 million for the foundation.

Linc went back to writing, Josh did some homework, and I did more research to cope with tomorrow's challenge, convincing TV news executives to accept the liar label and the Prediction Assessment. I sensed it was going to be a long slog.

"Josh, before you go, you want to look at some of what the talk shows are saying about Linc's proposals?"

"Sure."

On a whim, I started with Fox News. They showed a man holding a .357 magnum and shooting at a human silhouette at a firing range. "That looks to be their Lincoln story," Josh said.

"That's the one argument the NRA never thought of making," I said. "People need guns in case dead presidents rise up from the grave and say things they don't like. In that case you have to exercise your Second Amendment rights to prevent them from exercising their First Amendment rights. It makes perfect sense—if you're a psychopath."

On CNN a moderate minister suggested that perhaps Lincoln should be Tased multiple times rather than shot. Several panelists agreed that this would be the prudent and Christian thing to do.

"Wait just a minute," said the host. "Christianity is a religion based on love. Jesus said 'Love thy neighbor as thyself.' So how can you call this a Christian response?"

"But this zombie wants to edit the Bible," said one guest. "That can't be right. He wants to distort God's message."

"Lookin' good so far," Josh said.

On other channels, though, the news got better. The conversations were more about political reform than Bible edits. And almost everybody seemed to be for reform. Well, fine, although I hardly expected a panel to declare unanimously that the current system was perfect and nothing should be changed.

About ten minutes after Josh left, Livvie, Mom, Dad, and I heard a strange noise from outside. It sounded like a horde of people talking, murmuring, and even shouting. We looked out the window and saw at least five hundred people outside our building, some carrying signs reading, "God Haters Go to Hell! Now!" and "Pay as You Sow." One sign simply said "Scumbags!" Somehow they had penetrated the police barricade. We all went to the lobby to check out the furor, leaving Linc to his work.

I did a double take because I thought I saw Crockenstock at the head of the crowd, holding a bullhorn and wheeling one of his patented porta-potties, trailed by a TV crew. I knew I had a bad case of Crockenstock on my brain. Was this just another of my mad dreams? Alas, no. It was the Crock, and he was yelling, "This Lincoln is a disaster. He and his words belong in a toilet. Let's go get him and put him in the toilet.

"Are you with me?"

"YESSS!"

"Are you with me?"

"YESSS!"

"Where are we going to put him?"

"In the toilet, in the toilet, in the toilet," the crowd answered highmindedly. Because, really, what else would you do with the president ranked the best by historians of all political persuasions?

"What do we say to these God-haters?" someone yelled from the crowd.

"Haters gonna hate, haters gonna hate, haters gonna hate!"

A few moments later, these people rabidly opposed to hate began throwing raw eggs and rocks at our building.

"They live on five, they live on five," Crockenstock yelled.

We heard glass shattering. The crowd let out an enormous roar.

FBI agents Juan Morales and Edward Banks were now at the building's front door. They radioed their fellow agent to come down from the fifth floor, then called the cops and other agents for backup.

The police came quickly, as if summoned via Uber app. A scrum developed, with Crockenstock pushing the agents while he screamed, "Do you know how important I am? I am Crockenstock. I'm going to be the next president, then I'll be able to fire you."

Eventually, the agents and police took Crockenstock aside and tried to calm him down. After a slight pause, Crockenstock yelled, "Blitzkrieg!"

Inspired by the Teutonic cry, his minions threw dozens of additional eggs at the building. Agent Morales yelled, "Stop immediately or you'll all be arrested."

Crockenstock and his followers pressed forward.

"Get back or I'll arrest you," said Morales to Crockenstock.

"No you won't," said Crockenstock. "No one talks to me like that."

"Well, I do."

"I gave a million dollars to FBI director Comey's campaign."

"It's an appointive office, you stupid, fucking, racist douchebag. One more word and I'll smash your face in. Capiche?"

Enraged, Crockenstock rushed agent Morales and punched him in the face. Morales then smashed him in the head with his Glock. Crockenstock went down and Morales cuffed him, saying, "You're under arrest for assaulting a federal agent." Agent Morales pushed Crockenstock out the door and into the arms of two FBI agents who, I just realized, had been stationed one building down in what looked like a Verizon repair van.

"Book him and take him to Rikers," Morales said. "Try to put him in a cell with two three-hundred-pound bikers."

"Agent Morales," Crockenstock said, changing his tone completely, "I can give you a better apartment, rent free. I can get you out of that rat-infested hovel you inhabit in one of the unmentionable outer boroughs with your wretched excuse for a family. Please, we can settle this somehow."

"Add a charge of attempted bribery of a federal agent," Morales said. "Suggest bail of $5 billion. Let's see how much this lying cocksucker is really worth."

As the cops started to lead him away, Crockenstock screamed, "This is a nothing building. I live in a much nicer building. My worst toilet is nicer than this building."

The agents cuffed Crockenstock to the inside of his porta-potty and wheeled him away. Reluctantly, the crowd followed.

Then a swarm of neighbors descended, begging that we move Linc elsewhere. "He's going to be here only a few more days," I said.

Mrs. Dobson, the president of the co-op board, said the Linc issue might have to be addressed at the board level. Dad politely said he understood, then whispered to me that by the time the board did anything, Lincoln would have been spirited away.

"Please go back to your apartments, the show is over," said the super, trying valiantly, if belatedly, to restore order.

Upstairs, we saw that the rocks had smashed our dining room and living room windows. "I'll tape them with garbage bags," Mom said. "You go back down and help clean up. We owe that to our neighbors."

Oh, those anti-hate rallies can be so messy. It took almost an hour, but Livvie and I finally got most of the egg goop off the façade.

Livvie said, "Maybe this will finally be enough to trip up Crockenstock."

"Don't get your hopes up," Dad said. "He could buy off the entire southern district and eastern district attorneys if he set his mind to it. It's not as if we can rely on his scruples to stop him."

Gee, that was depressing. I hoped it wasn't true. Once again, we turned on the TV to discover that what we had just witnessed was the top story in the nation. This was getting ridiculous. "You know it won't always be like this," Dad said, as if reading my mind.

"I know, but I just needed to see video confirmation that I wasn't hallucinating when I saw Crockenstock wheeled away in a toilet." Indeed, there he was, screaming at the people who had cuffed him to his toilet. "Livvie, watch this. There's a lesson here for all of us. When you think you may be about to commit multiple crimes, don't bring along a camera crew." Crockenstock's attempted bribery was captured beautifully on film.

Linc had been concentrating so deeply on his writing that he missed the riot. "You didn't hear the chanting and the crashing glass?" Livvie said.

"No."

We filled Linc in. "So he was really led away handcuffed to a toilet?" he said. "Well done."

"Dad, can a felon be elected president?" I said.

"Yes. He just isn't allowed to vote for himself in New York until his parole is over."

"Doesn't that seem a little ass-backward?"

"At the moment, and given the person any prohibition would apply to, it certainly does. I think it fair to say that the framers and state legislators did not anticipate Crockenstock."

Chapter 15

I WOKE UP AT 5:30 to the sound of a car backfiring. Then a second car. Then a third.

I started to run toward Linc's room, but Dad was ahead of me and yelled, "Stay back! That was rifle fire!" Dad stayed down, almost crawling along the floor to get to Linc.

We found Linc on the floor, shielded by his desk. Blood from his right cheek was dripping on the rug. "Oh my God, you're hurt," Dad said from the floor of the hallway.

"The first shot grazed my check," Linc said. "Then I took cover."

"I'll go tell the FBI," Dad said, crawling past Linc's doorway.

"The timing was really bad," Linc said, "because I think I had just figured out a way to discuss my Bible views without making people so upset, to show them my opinions are really more about politics than religion. I take it that fellow out there with the rifle was upset."

"You are a logical man, Linc. What did you just figure out?"

"Oh, I'm still working on it. You know I don't like to say things until I'm good and ready."

"And that approach served you so well on *60 Minutes*!"

"I said what I wanted to say. I guess I knew some people would reach for their guns. I just never thought it would be so many."

"I feel so stupid that we left you in a room with windows. I'm sorry. I'm very sorry."

"Don't be. I went out yesterday and nothing happened. So I'll spend my remaining time on Earth with a bandaged cheek. Your sister always said I needed a makeover."

"Even Livvie couldn't have meant this."

Dad came back with two FBI agents. "We've sent for a medical team to take care of your wound here," said Morales. "We don't want you leaving the building right now with an active shooter outside."

The agents helped bring Linc to the windowless dining room. We brought towels and a bowl of warm water. Linc held a towel to his face to stanch the blood. He reminded me of a photo of a wounded Civil War soldier, his face bandaged with rags.

Of course, I also thought of another time when someone had taken a shot at Linc. He and Mary had been watching the battle of Fort Stevens from a parapet when a surgeon next to the president had been hit. Still, Lincoln had stood tall. "Get down, you fool!" said a young captain named Oliver Wendell Holmes Jr., addressing his president. Holmes, of course, went on to become a distinguished Supreme Court justice.

The medical team gave Linc twelve stitches and bandaged him properly. "Can you cancel today's events, Mr. President?" Morales said.

"I don't really see how I can," Linc said. "I have to try to convince the TV news executives to consider some of our reforms. The Masons could undoubtedly do a good job presenting the ideas, but I suspect the executives want to hear them from the horse's mouth. Or some part of the horse. And tomorrow night I give the speech at Cooper Union, and that's important in a different way. I must keep my promises."

"You're a brave man, sir," said Morales.

Linc smiled. "I never had much physical fear. And, you know, you have even less when you know your days are as numbered as mine are."

As things settled down, we caught up with the Crockenstock story on TV. The turd mogul had indeed spent the night in a cell at Riker's, with his new biker friends Jumbo and Ironballs. This morning he had been arraigned on charges of assaulting a federal agent, attempted bribery of a federal agent, and inciting a riot. The judge cited Crockenstock, who twice asked her to apologize for interrupting him, for contempt of court sixteen times. "Sir," she said, "I never truly appreciated the meaning of contempt until I met you." His attorney paid the $72,000 in fines and the bail money solely in change, the last $5,000 in pennies.

"Why did you do that?" reporters asked Crockenstock.

"Because I can. Money talks, bullshit walks."

As if to demonstrate the truth of that last phrase, Crockenstock sauntered away, temporarily a free man. And now he was at a press conference, trying desperately to spin his indictments. "I will be attending the ugly zombie's lecture at Cooper Union," he said. "I may well heckle him. As a citizen I have the right to say what I want."

"But you and your supporters don't feel others have the right to heckle you," said a reporter. "That's why there have been eighty-five deaths at your rallies thus far."

"You don't know what you're talking about, you moron," Crockenstock lied. "All those people—every single one—died of natural causes. The joy of the rallies just proved too much for them. And if you keep saying and printing untrue things like that, we're going to sue you and jail you when I become president. Let's see how you like your time in a cell with men named Jumbo and Ironballs."

I ditched school again to attend Linc's noon meeting with the news execs at a large NBC news conference room at 30 Rock. Some thanked him for coming despite his wound. Linc shook their hands graciously.

Then Linc sat up at the front of the room with people from,

and affiliated with, his foundation. The news execs sat at long tables, behind signs bearing their names. There were no cameras in the room.

Almost immediately, it became apparent there was a skunk at this particular garden party, and his name was Jeff Smeeport, the ruddy-faced executive vice president of Fox News.

"What is truth?" he shouted early on.

"You would ask that, Jeff," said Sam Ritter from NBC News.

"What's a fact?" Smeeport continued.

"Haven't seen one lately?" said Anna Nelson from CBS News.

"No, I'm serious," said Smeeport. "There are lots of shades of gray here, and I think we have to be very careful about what we agree to, if anything. What if Crockenstock has a Lincoln Liar label on NBC but not on CBS?"

"It's hard to imagine that ever occurring," said CBS's Nelson.

"Okay, perhaps Crockenstock is a bad example. What if Chris Christie came on and said, 'Look, I'm a nice guy—'"

"Liar!" yelled a news guy several rows back.

"Liar, liar, liar, liar," came a hostile chorus from news executives around the room. They all sounded like New Jersey residents who commuted via the George Washington Bridge.

"Would he even think of saying such a thing?" said MSNBC's Elliott Lee.

"Surely we can imagine an example," Smeeport said. "What if Lenny Plotnik said that we could easily pay for all of his glorious programs, but our math suggested otherwise? Is he lying or not lying or do we just not have enough information?"

"Ladies and gentlemen, if I may address you for a moment," said Linc, standing up and moving closer to the news execs. He seemed to make eye contact with everybody. "First, I thank you all for coming. For many reasons, if you agree to do this at all, I think you should start with the most outrageous examples, where there is absolutely no gray area. If our Lincoln Liar designations are seen as inaccurate or politically motivated, this program will fail, and it will fail quickly."

"President Lincoln," said Smeeport, "what would you have us do if a guest has repeatedly lied about an issue before but hems and haws and fudges on air? What carries the day?"

"I don't think that person would merit the liar designation for that appearance," Linc said, "but you're asking an important question. The goal is not to brand people as liars. It is to discourage lying. It is, moreover, to encourage truth-telling. Where things get really tricky is when someone like Senator Arrogandez indicates through vague language and choice of speaking venues that he believes in creationism rather than evolution, but doesn't come right out and say it. But he uses a kind of code that communicates the message very clearly to people who have such views.

"I deplore such political chicanery, but I don't think the Lincoln Liar program can police it effectively. Some politicians simply do not want to get pinned down, and the liar label is too blunt an instrument to change that behavior."

This was all interesting, but my mind kept wandering. How was Linc going to calm the fury unleashed by his Bible amendment strategy? I'm glad he didn't ask me for a solution. I didn't have one.

The news directors found it easier to accept the Prediction Assessment (PA) score. Isn't it interesting that it is more socially acceptable to point out that someone is wrong all the time and had been for years than to call that person a liar? The news honchos clearly thought the first category of alleged error was data-driven, whereas the second was more of a moral judgment. Our initial statistical run showed that virtually all politicians had forecasting records that lay somewhere between "abysmal" and "you've got to be kidding," but Republicans, because of their ability to anticipate flaming ruins with persistent regularity, fared worst.

Linc tried to explain the two forms of error were more closely related than his audience might have assumed. "My decades of experience in politics have taught me that the ability to foresee the future effects of a particular piece of legislation or judicial decision is a gift not widely dispersed among the political class. But does that stop such people from making predictions? Of course not.

"What always bothered me was the intellectual dishonesty of the errant predictions. Someone who wanted less spending on internal improvements would say that such spending would bankrupt the state and cause Illinois to fall into the sea—a geographic improbability. A person in favor would say additional spending would lead to astonishing growth and that, without it, no business would relocate to Illinois for the next century and all our children would be barefoot and hungry.

"There is a difference between a rhetorical flourish and a statement that the speaker knows cannot possibly come true. I tried always to keep this in mind, even if some of my colleagues did not. And I came to know which of my colleagues could be relied upon to exaggerate all the way up to the line of falsehood and beyond. Some politicians are so set on scaring the living daylights out of people with their predictions that they never take the time to try to get any of them right. Theirs are more like creepy campfire stories rather than good faith predictions.

"So I am glad you like the prediction score. I like it, too. I just happen to think that a senator whose predictions are correct 1 percent of the time is, morally speaking, exactly the same as a senator who has earned a liar label. I hope you and the American public come to see it this way as well.

"To my mind, the two ideas should work together well. A politician will want to raise his prediction score. Perhaps he or she will want to use it against a rival in a campaign. Someone who has been tarred with a liar label will want to be rid of it as soon as possible. Of course, there will be exceptions. A candidate might decide that receiving money from oil interests is more important than telling the truth about climate change. With this new system in place, we will see how well that works out for them. If you agree to highlight the officials' three largest donors by industry, we might see our elected officials more in tune with the needs of constituents rather than their largest donors.

"Verbal precision is important, and that reminds me of a story."

Oh, Linc and his stories. How I was going to miss them.

"During the War of 1812, which took place when I was three, some young women were making belts with engraved mottoes for their male friends to take into battle. When one of the young women suggested 'Liberty or Death!' her soldier friend said the phrase was 'rather strong.' Couldn't she make it 'Liberty or Crippled' instead?

"We want voters to respect how we label politicians or assess their predictive powers. When I was a politician, I cared about some words much more than others. I was insulted so many times I long ago lost count. I have been called an 'imbecile' on the Senate floor. Oh well, it came with the territory. But if I had ever come to be known as 'Dishonest Abe,' *that* would have bothered me.

"I've told my hosts, the Mason family, that the nation has been through more divisive times than these and survived. We survived the Civil War: we can survive this. But I don't know a time when certain industrial interests, such as the Koch brothers, have done more to misinform the nation by funding candidates they know will lie to the American people. I know it's a lot to ask of you to sit there and listen to a man who's been dead for more than a century discuss an issue—in this case, climate change—that he knew nothing about until a week ago. But I've concluded the evidence is overwhelming. The danger is clear, and many politicians are lying about it. That's why we need liar labels now. It is urgent.

"So I hope you'll consider these tools carefully and put them to good use."

"Mr. President, may I ask you a question?" said Chuck Mangano from ABC News.

"Of course."

"We are not in the habit of editorializing, and some of what you are proposing makes me nervous. We don't want our coverage to sway elections. We want to cover the news."

"Ah, if only it were so simple. Let me make several points. First, you have all started running fact-checking features after debates or other public forums. You may not use the word 'liar,' but you do use the words 'true' and 'false.' So you have already taken steps in this direction. I maintain these fact-checking efforts would do far more good for the nation if they happened as close to real time as possible, so the liar would have his or her words undermined from the start.

"Second, in your efforts to fulfill your role in our democracy, you are all unwitting conduits of outrageous deceit some of the time. Politicians are adept at using you. And your excessively good manners have become a serious liability when you have on one of your programs a guest like Ronald Crockenstock. If your interviewers refuse to call him a liar to his face, the exposure you provide simply enhances his power. He lies very, very often, and you have a duty to report this. If you do not change your behavior and he is elected president, history will judge you as having been complicit in his rise to power.

"Finally, I have no problem with ABC News and Fox News disagreeing about what is a lie. This will inevitably happen. You do not have to accept the decisions of the Lincoln Foundation. Over time, though, I hope that, if the foundation does its job properly, it may become a competitive disadvantage to ignore the Lincoln Liar designation, the Prediction Assessment score, and the top donor information.

"I always thought that the greatest challenge for a leader in a democratic society is to educate public opinion, and I believe that this is also your challenge. I hope you do it well."

"But what if we call someone a liar and he sues us and wins?" said Jack Beacham of CNN.

Dad's lawyer friend, Walt McCall, the foundation's chief counsel, rose to answer. "The Lincoln Foundation will indemnify you completely," he said. "If we make a mistake, we will pay for everything, including attorney's fees. But, remember, the people involved will all be public figures. To win a libel case, they would have to prove 'actual malice,' which means knowing that what was said was false or acting with reckless disregard of whether it was true or not. The people at the Lincoln Foundation will be obsessed with credibility. Any mistakes at the start could cripple the program forever. The foundation will always be careful, but especially at the outset. We will begin by focusing exclusively on outlandish distortions of the facts. That alone should keep us very busy."

Professor Philip Tetlock and FiveThirtyEight's Nate Silver then explained some of the intricacies of the PA score. Tetlock said his research showed that the commitment to self-improvement was a leading predictor of forecasting success.

Both men noted that you could increase your score by occasionally resisting the urge to make a prediction. Avoiding a prediction was far better than offering a lousy one. Alas, the irresponsible prediction had become such a staple of political rhetoric that voters had long ago stopped penalizing politicians for being ludicrously wrong. Perhaps, Tetlock said, scientific monitoring could change that.

In their attempts to define precision, Tetlock and Silver naturally indicated how the system could be gamed. If you said a tax increase would lead to the destruction of the United States, but didn't say *when* that catastrophe would occur, that would not count as an incorrect prediction if the country were still on its feet six months from now. On the other hand, a politician who never had the guts to make an unhedged prediction would never get anything wrong but would never get anything right either. He would have a batting average of .000, which might be as unimpressive in the political world as it is on the baseball diamond.

By the time the meeting was over, the foundation had come closer to reaching agreements with the networks. I couldn't swear that was going to happen, but it seemed likely. Linc was upbeat.

"I'm not sure that this calls for more fountain-dancing," he said, "but I think we did well. We might never convince Fox News, though."

"You never know how that will play out," Dad said. "If Fox is the only holdout, they may be shamed into going along with us eventually.

Then again, many of their viewers would probably dispute the foundation's determinations anyway, so I wouldn't worry about it too much."

Once we were back home, Linc joined us for a quick dinner, then went to work on his book and Cooper Union speech. After an hour he knocked on my door.

"Henry, I appreciate everything you've said about me as a writer, but there is one thing you cannot say."

"What?"

"That I am a fast one. I worked on my 1860 Cooper Union speech for four months. The book is coming along, but I'm writing it so quickly I fear it won't be any good."

"May I tell you a story?"

"Of course."

"After serving two terms as president, your favorite general, Ulysses S. Grant, joined a business started by a New York swindler. The business blew up, leaving Grant penniless. Doctors then diagnosed him with terminal throat cancer. His friend Mark Twain, the great writer, encouraged him to write his autobiography to help support his family after his death. So Grant, often in great pain, worked furiously, sometimes writing fifty or sixty pages a day. He finished the book five days before his death, just as Lee surrendered at Appomattox five days before you were shot. History can be strange that way."

"But was Grant's book any good?"

"Many people, including my father, consider it a masterpiece. And, after Twain hired Union veterans to sell the book door to door, it become an enormous financial success as well."

"Henry, you've done it again. You are good at encouragement bordering on coercion." He smiled. "I can go back to work now."

"Anything I can do to help?"

He asked me to find articles and speeches about religious people who had criticized parts of the Bible. Oh no, he was going to step in it yet again.

Chapter 16

I WENT TO SCHOOL again, taking a stab at having an ordinary day. Josh came up and said, "My father would like to talk to you about this wartime consigliere position. He wants something in writing. It's not that he doesn't trust you. He doesn't trust anybody. And, as you know, he's a devout believer in Murphy's Law."

"If it will help you at home, I'll do it. My intent is sincere. Of course, it's contingent upon many things. Reaching the age of thirty-five, for one thing."

"As you said, you have many enemies, certainly a lot more than you had before you met President Lincoln. But I still think it's two to one you make it to thirty-five."

"Gee, thanks."

The day was fairly normal, but at the beginning of lunch I felt the need for an adulation fix. So I went over to the long table of ass-holes—it's so nice they all hang together—and answered some questions and told some quick stories. I made vague promises, then had lunch with Josh and Ethan. Ethan had started acting decidedly insecure around me. He knew my status had changed and his number one rank with Josh was in jeopardy. I wish I could tell you I didn't enjoy it. Well, I didn't. I *loved* it.

Back home, I heard Linc going through his Cooper Union speech. I thought of listening at his door but decided that would be cheating. I'd hear his words soon enough.

After dinner, our three original FBI agents put us all in a van— another group of agents were in the black SUV ahead of us—and drove us to Cooper Union, which is on Astor Place in Greenwich Village. The Great Hall at Cooper Union has 855 seats and is occasionally used for large classes, such as introductory physics, a class I pray I never have to take.

When Lincoln made his historic speech here on February 27, 1860, the one-year-old hall looked quite different. It had more than twice as many seats—eighteen hundred—and was the largest auditorium in Manhattan. Fifteen hundred people paid twenty-five cents apiece to hear Abraham Lincoln speak about how a majority of the founders had, on different occasions, cast votes indicating their belief that the federal government had the right to limit the spread of slavery. The Gettysburg Address may be the most moving and the most beautiful speech ever given by an American, but it is not the most important. The "right makes might" speech Lincoln delivered at the Great Hall in 1860 altered history.

He arrived at the hall as an extreme dark horse in the race for the Republican presidential nomination, far behind Seward, Chase, and Bates in recognition, respect, and power. Had the speech not been a stunning success, Lincoln never would have become president in 1861. The person who instead became president might not have fought the Civil War or might have abandoned the awful task before its successful conclusion. Had the two sections of America remained separate, we might not have been strong enough to help win the First and Second World Wars.

Since Lincoln's 1860 speech, the stage has been moved from the south end of the auditorium to the north, but some things have not changed. Dignitaries who speak from the stage still use the same lectern that Lincoln used and have included Presidents Grant, Cleveland, Theodore Roosevelt, Taft, and Obama—before they became president—and Wilson and Clinton while they were in office.

We stood with Linc on the stage as we watched famous faces take their seats. We saw New York's governor Andrew Cuomo and the city's mayor, Bill de Blasio. Happily, the state's two senators, Chuck Schumer and Kirsten Gillibrand, thus considerably reducing the chance of physical violence. I saw former mayor Mike Bloomberg, that political rarity, a genuine straight-shooter; police chief William Bratton; our congresswoman, Carolyn Maloney; Nora and Bart Blitzen; and seated together, remarkably, Bono and Henry Kissinger, looking over sheet music. (Bruce Springsteen was to Bono's right, but that actually made sense, since they liked and admired each other, although the look on Springsteen's face seemed to say, "I'm one seat away from Henry Kissinger. That's so fucked up.") Nearby sat an epidemic of billionaires, conquerors of the worlds of Wall Street, real estate, media, and entertainment. Two grizzled men who headed a pillaging conglomerate sat with their astonishingly young wives, who looked as if they had recently been plucked from Columbia or NYU.

"Hey, Dad, weren't they in your intro American history class last year?" I said. He smiled and tried not to laugh.

Steven Spielberg, the director of *Lincoln*, sat next to Sam Waterston, star of Gore Vidal's *Lincoln* and performer of Lincoln's Cooper Union speech in this very hall in 2004. Most necks turned when a glut of Crockenstocks entered. There was the remarkable man himself, his wife Extravaganza (sorry, I mean Exalta; the important thing is the name begins with Ex), and assorted children of wildly different ages, along with a retinue of paid grovelers. How cozy. They were seated second row, center. Great, just what Linc needed, the threat of rabid heckling, up close and personal.

One FBI agent stood on stage, another at the back of the auditorium, and the third in the middle. We assumed the others were out front. Security people examined bags at the entrance, which, since 9/11, now happened at any New York event more formal than a three-year-old's birthday party. The thought of terror was a daily presence, if not necessarily a daily concern. Here, as at the Beacon Theatre, security people confiscated bottles of water, fearful that the plastic bottles could serve as projectiles that would . . . would what exactly? No one seemed to know. If you bought a bottle of Dasani purified tap water at the Beacon, they took the cap off and kept it. Which meant that you had to spend the entire concert worrying that your water was going to spill on your lap. Clearly, someone thought that giving you the cap would weaponize the bottle. When I had a moment, I would Google how many rock stars had ever been incapacitated by flying purified tap water.

As we got ready to take our seats on the stage, I was glad that we weren't seated behind one of the hall's eighteen white columns that partially obscured the view from some seats. Suddenly, something caught my eye behind one of the columns. It was shiny. But there was something else behind the column. A large person, aiming a gun at Linc.

Without thinking, I lunged to my right to intercept the bullet headed for Linc's heart. I felt my right shoulder explode. I went down. As I registered the enormous pain, like being stabbed with a hot knife, I heard screaming. Then what seemed like dozens of people fell on top of me. Everything went black.

Chapter 17

I DREAMED A HITMAN had entered my hospital room and was about to smother me with a pillow. I woke up terrified. The room was full of people, and for a second I thought they were all holding pillows. It took me a moment to make out their faces. "Oh, look, he's awake," Mom said. Then I realized I was surrounded by my family. And lots of flowers. And Josh. Everyone, even Livvie, seemed happy to see me awake and vaguely conscious.

"I thought I told you to duck," Josh said. "You pretty much did the opposite. And now you're even more famous than you were two days ago."

"You're the most famous thirteen-year-old on the planet," Livvie said.

I heard the words but they didn't mean much. I was pretty drugged.

"Henry," said my father, "would you like to hear what President Obama wrote you?"

"He wrote me? Why would he do that?"

"He sent a telegram. It says,

'Dear Henry,

The kindness you showed President Lincoln and your remarkable bravery in trying to protect him should serve as an inspiration to all Americans, young and old. When I met President Lincoln, he told me a lot about you. I was impressed then and I'm more impressed now. Thank you for your service to the nation. When you recover, Michelle and I would love to welcome you and your family to the White House.

Sincerely,

Barack Obama.'"

"Henry, it looks like you'll be getting to the White House ahead of schedule," Mom said. "You won't have to wait until you're thirty-five."

"The president's note is very nice," I said, "but what exactly happened? And where is Linc?" But I knew the answer before I finished uttering the question. My country had done it again.

They said that after the first bullet hit me, more shots came from two directions, hitting Linc in the head and neck. He died before they could get him into an ambulance.

"He was assassinated *again*? This country is sicker than I thought. The greatest president in history comes back again to try to heal things—and they kill him. The bastards kill him. They want to continue preaching hatred so much that they have to kill him. God damn them! God damn them all!" And, again, I started crying.

Both my parents came closer to comfort me. Mom put her hand on my head. Dad touched me on the arm. Eventually I was ready to listen to what they had to say.

"They killed one of the shooters and wounded the other one,"

Dad said. "He's talking. They were members of a God Squad from South Carolina."

"How appropriate," I said. "South Carolina, the home of Fort Sumter, where the Civil War started and which Linc always used to misspell. Great writer, lousy speller." Then I almost lost it again. "They couldn't have let him stay here for three more days? Just three more lousy days? Americans are given a gift and they fuckin' kill it."

My surgeon, Dr. Answorth Allen, entered. He was the team physician for the New York Knicks and had been the team doctor for my beloved Mets. I was obviously in good hands at the Hospital for Special Surgery.

"Dr. Allen, will I ever pitch again?"

"Well, you'll probably never have the velocity you would have had before the damage. You might be able to become a knuckleballer."

"Oh, on that note, Henry," said my father, "you got a telegram from R. A. Dickey offering to teach you the knuckleball when you're ready."

My trancelike feeling returned. Dickey had won the Cy Young award with the Mets in 2012, the first Met to do so since Dwight Gooden in 1985. So this was like Eric Clapton offering me guitar lessons.

"I put that on your to-do list," Mom said. "But physical therapy comes first."

"Also on the to-do list?"

"Absolutely."

Dad swung us back to politics. "The FBI has started arresting other God Squad members for conspiracy," he said. "There may have been as many as fifty church-sponsored hitmen dispatched to kill President Lincoln."

The surviving Cooper Union shooter said he'd acted on orders from Lee Chesney, the televangelist who headed the Groveside megachurch in Charleston, South Carolina. Chesney presided over a congregation of thirty-five thousand and reached millions more through his weekly televised services. He was one of the nation's leading exemplars of religious faith and the redemptive power of lovingkindness. And now murder.

Later, the feds would give Rev. Chesney a stark choice. Plead guilty and endure life in prison without parole, or go to trial and face the death penalty under federal terrorism statutes. Then they added a kicker. If he took the plea, he would spend most of his time in solitary confinement, and, when not in solitary, he would not be allowed to speak to any fellow inmates or have any visitors. The American Civil Liberties Union filed suit, saying this was a violation of both the First Amendment and the Eighth Amendment, which bars cruel and unusual punishment.

But the ACLU lost, as judges concluded that Rev. Chesney's brand of conversation and the repeated threats he made to anyone who objected to any part of the Bible would by definition represent an imminent risk to human life.

President Lincoln's second death changed the world. Taken together, the knowledge that a man of the cloth had ordered the assassination, that dozens of his brethren had sent hired guns as well, and that a man so beloved was assassinated for a second time just days before he would have taken his peaceful leave of Earth helped diminish the power of fundamentalists.

And so did their behavior at Linc's funeral and the long train ride that followed. While millions of Americans lined train tracks to see Linc's body again transported from Washington to Springfield, Illinois, thousands of fundamentalists came to protest, shouting that Lincoln the blasphemer deserved to die.

But a strange thing happened. In interviews with protesters, some reporters asked the question Linc might have posed. Do you believe every word in the Bible? When a protester said yes, the reporters often turned Lincoln's logic against them, asking why he or she didn't kill people who worked on the Sabbath. "I'm working on the Sabbath right now," one famous TV reporter told several interview subjects. "Why don't you kill me?"

No one effectively explained the mystery of why they swore by certain passages of the Bible while completely ignoring others. Not so long ago, when someone told a reporter "It is God's will," that tended to end the discussion. Now reporters often responded by saying, "That doesn't stop it from being a crime."

The poll numbers of fundamentalist politicians plunged. As Senator Arrogandez continued to insist that God's law always outranked the U.S. judicial system, his poll numbers cratered. Even in Louisiana his support vaporized. Journalists speculated he would be unable to get the Republican nomination in his next Senate race.

Then the *New York Times* ran its series on how fundamentalist Christians, Muslims, and Jews all treated women as second-class citizens. The series won a Pulitzer and led other papers to question formerly sacrosanct practices.

A flock of "asterisk" and "fundamentalist lite" congregations using amended Bibles sprang up. Even though attendance at fundamentalist churches fell, the number of people attending all religious services increased following Linc's reappearance, reversing a trend.

Soon worshipers held more interfaith services. The "inclusion/exclusion" doctrine, so expertly, if chillingly, articulated by Senator Arrogandez, was widely ridiculed. Instead of focusing on their differences, Americans began stressing common beliefs. The shift, which some cynics labeled a "Kumbaya moment," reminded me of what occurred during the Christmas Truce of 1914 during World War I, when troops fighting each other paused, came out of their trenches, and talked and sang together and even exchanged gifts. America seemed to be enjoying a cessation of hostilities.

In late 2016 a Gallup Poll hit like an earthquake. It showed that only 20 percent of American voters opposed abortion *and* considered homosexuality a sin. This meant that what had been the Republican base was no longer the base. It was now a fringe group, albeit a very large one. It was widely said that candidates for the Republican nomination who actively courted this group would be doomed in a general election. In fact, there was now a decent chance that the Republican presidential nominee in 2020 would be pro-choice.

Finally, polls showed that 75 percent of registered Republicans said they believed in human-caused climate change. Deniers became toxic candidates. Soon it became clear that getting even a dollar from a fossil fuel company was political death for any national candidate. The Koch brothers began concentrating on small-town city council races. Most of the candidates they sought to back turned down their money.

And how did Crockenstock fare in this environment? Badly. After being sentenced to four months in prison, plus two months, in advance, for bad behavior, he entered the minimum security prison at Pensacola, Florida. "It's a dump," he said, "even uglier than the place where the Mason family lives." Fellow prisoners beat him only four times during his six-month stay. The Las Vegas betting line had predicted almost daily beatings. "Beating on him wasn't much fun," said one of his cellmates. "He just whined so much."

After Crockenstock's conviction, managers of construction sites began removing his pay toilets and renting no-fee porta-potties instead. Some restaurants and hotels put up signs inviting Pay as You Go "refugees" to use their free restrooms. In an impressive display of consumer power, tens of millions of people boycotted Pay as You Go, and Crockenstock's empire quickly collapsed into bankruptcy.

Shed no tears for him, however. His new book, *Down the Toilet: How to Turn Success into Failure*, was a best-seller ("the greatest book ever written about failure," he crowed), and, following his release, he made a nice living giving speeches to white supremacist groups. But not nice enough. His wife Exalta, eyeing greener pastures, divorced him.

The foundation settled its suit against Marshall Wendell for $50 million, which was both a moral victory and a financial coup. The suit against Parasites was progressing well, so well that the site offered to retract its charges if the foundation dropped the suit. We declined. The editor said, "What are you trying to do, bankrupt us?"

"Yes," said my father. "We think of it as a public service."

TV news outlets adopted the Lincoln Liar labels on some occasions, but there seemed less need after Linc's murder. TV news also introduced information on the candidates' top three donors and the Prediction Assessment scores, but, intriguingly, new political predictions began to seem less apocalyptic. Livvie, our trend expert, said it had become unfashionable to declare that one's political opponent was determined to eviscerate the Constitution and cast the country into centuries of darkness.

The Lincoln Foundation launched its Pay as You Grow reading program, as well as thousands of political reading groups for young people around the country. Livvie smiled when Amazon released her "Liar" song collection as a CD and promoted it like crazy.

Hundreds of media outlets wanted to interview me, so I turned to Mom for advice. She picked the four I accepted. I confess, it was hard to stop. For the first few days, I loved the attention and my new identity as the young hero who, for a short time, was a friend of Abe Lincoln. Everyone, even Josh, wanted to talk about my heroism and hear stories about my pal Linc.

Even when I was alone with Josh, he kept referring to me as a hero until I told him to cut it out. "You know, I'm still the same person I was before."

"No, that's where you're wrong. This has changed your life forever. You can't go back." He was in full pronouncement mode.

"But I want to go back, you know, some."

"Can't be done. You're like a superhero now. You can say, 'Oh, I'm just Clark Kent or Bruce Wayne or Peter Parker,' but you can't renounce your superpower."

He was on to something. My classmates now treated me as if I were a kind of magical object, something that should be rubbed for luck. People were too impressed ever to mention the obvious, that my act of heroism hadn't protected Linc or anyone else from harm. They had endless questions and seemed fascinated—with the new me, that is.

"But can't I just be a better, more interesting version of my old self instead of someone who's been totally transformed?" I said to Josh.

"You can try, but what you did is going to follow you forever. If you were older, people would be telling you to run for Congress or something."

"Josh, there's something I want to show you." From my closet I pulled out a copy of the Gettysburg Address, handwritten by Linc and dedicated to me. It was signed "A. Lincoln, 2015."

"He left you quite a goodie bag. That's a pretty valuable piece of paper. Aw, I knew you were in this for the money all along."

"Josh, my former consigliere, I'm going to kill you." Then we just started laughing. We went and sat down in the family room.

"So where should I go to school next year?"

"I bet you could get into Harvard, Yale, or Stanford right now. Granted, it would be very, very, very early decision, but you could give it a shot."

"Nah," I said, "I just want to find a good school that's either close to Forbish Milton or near where you live."

"Stalker."

"Josh, you are such an asshole."

"I know. And, mind you, it takes work."

I continued to see Gillian outside of school. I really liked her. We kissed and I liked that too. But she told me that thirteen is too young to have a boyfriend. Now we're friends who make out sometimes. "Oh, that's so nice," said Josh, with mock sincerity. "You're friends with itsy-bitsy benefits."

Given the inanities of the 2016 presidential campaign, Gillian was surprised that I could still consider entering politics someday. I told her that if you left the field to the Wall Street bootlickers, the deeply-inbred scions of wealth, the profoundly corrupt, the 24/7 esteemed-senators-addicted-to-nubile-intern-cavity-searches whose disregarded wives have turned into the Pat Nixon walking dead, the closeted, wide-stanced Republican gay-bashers, the Chuck Schumer God-I-haven't-been-on-TV-yet-today-and-I-just-can't-stand-it media sluts, and the Kanye West I-can't-handle-my-life-but-the-presidency-sounds-interesting lunatics, then we'd get the kind of government we deserve.

"But given everything that's changed since President Lincoln was here," I said, "it might actually be possible to be in politics without losing your soul."

With that thought in mind, I asked Livvie what I should do with my brand.

"Are you serious?" she said, beaming.

"I am."

"Well, first of all, that was super brilliant what you did, jumping in front of that bullet. And with the cameras rolling and everything and all the celebrities there. That will probably get you five hundred million views on YouTube."

Then she went on—and on and on—about all the different things I could do now with Facebook, Instagram, Twitter, SnapChat, and the rest of the social media arsenal. She was definitely in her realm, and many of her ideas seemed good. And she was really excited about my running for president someday.

As she was speaking, though, it occurred to me that one thing I disliked about social media was that many messages were designed to appear casual or informative, but they were really something else entirely. Their purpose was to sell, court fame, generate clicks and page-views, and remind people that you existed—so they might do something that helped you. Some of what you saw on social media was like politics at its worst, one disingenuous act after another, a kind of ritualized insincerity. You posted things because you wanted something, like a kid writing up a list for Santa. You told people you "liked" them so they would "like" you back.

Dad finished Linc's book for him and, within a year, wrote his own. Both did very well. And, as you can tell, I wrote the story of the most amazing time of my life.

Dad said he was very proud of how I'd acted with Linc. "And I don't just mean the getting shot part. That was very brave and also pretty crazy, risking your life for someone who was going to go back into the ground in three days.

"But what I really want to say is that President Lincoln liked you for some very good reasons. Remember that, especially on bad days when it seems the world is conspiring against you."

For the first time in my life, my parents actively tried to make me feel less pressured. "Don't feel obligated to become president or even go into politics just because of how President Lincoln felt about you," Mom said. "Your time with Lincoln should be a great positive in your life, not a burden. The world is full of people who buckled under the weight of outsized expectations. Look at what Senator Arrogandez's parents did to him."

"I know. But at least the man is now getting some good bookings in the Catskills."

My ten days with Linc were the best of my life because I knew exactly what my purpose was at every moment. Do you know what a weird, wonderful feeling that is for a thirteen-year-old? I was there to serve as Linc's guide to our world and help him try to fix it. Feeling so determined was new for me—and I liked it.

A lot. That had to be one of the keys to happiness, having a strong sense of what mattered and then working hard at it. So now I knew I wanted to do that. Above all, I wanted to be useful.

In a matter of weeks, the press and the public gave me more than a lifetime's worth of acclaim. I no longer felt the need for any adulation fixes. In fact, I was close to overdosing already.

Now, for the first time in my life, I felt almost mellow. I started meditating. I no longer worried about what would happen next. When the time came, I'd figure out what to do. Me, confident—what a thought! And if my first choice turned out to be a mistake—if, say, I went to law school and absolutely hated it—then I'd try plan B.

One of the articles about me was headlined "Young Man in a Hurry," but I really wasn't in a hurry at all. As Tolstoy said, "The strongest of all warriors are these two—Time and Patience." That's from *War and Peace*, a book I have *not* read. I cribbed the quotation from *Bartlett's*. Did you think I'm weird or something? You think I read books all the time?

I stayed focused on my R. A. Dickey knuckleball lessons, which were going well. As for politics, I wasn't sure I'd ever be serious about it. Maybe I would try someday, but I just didn't know. Yes, I had a helluva campaign poster, but that wouldn't determine my fate.

But I did become president of the ninth grade at Montague Wilson (winning on a platform stressing divestiture from oil company stocks) and a member of a political discussion group sponsored by the Lincoln Foundation. I kept working to improve people's knowledge of climate change. "You know," said Josh, "you should really be exploiting your fame for sex." Sorry, Josh, that wasn't on my to-do list.

Every day, I looked up at the sky and imagined I saw Linc's face, usually smiling down on me. And I thought of his words: "With malice toward none, with charity for all, with firmness in the right as God gives us to see the right, let us strive to finish the work we are in, to bind up the nation's wounds, to care for him who shall have borne the battle and for his widow and his orphan, to do all which may achieve and cherish a just and lasting peace among ourselves and with all nations."

I could hear him say, "Are you quoting me to me *again*?"

So it seemed. Thanks to Abraham Lincoln, I had been given fame far beyond my merits. People ascribed virtues to me that I only wished I had. The least I could do was to try to transform these generous misperceptions into work that mattered. I would strive to be useful all the days of my life.

"What, no quote from Shakespeare?" Linc's voice said in my head.

"Okay, okay," I said.

> "He was a man, take him for all in all.
> I shall not look upon his like again."

"That's better," Linc said.

Indeed, it was better. Much about the country was better. There was a reasonable chance that the better angels of our nature might prevail.

Acknowledgments

I want to express my gratitude to David Greenstein and Kim Newman of Cooper Union for providing essential information about the Great Hall, including a guided tour. Thanks to Harold Holzer for his inspiring book, Lincoln at Cooper Union: The Speech That Made Abraham Lincoln President. And thanks to Sam Waterston for his vivid reenactment of Lincoln's Cooper Union address. You can see it on YouTube—and you should.

I appreciate the help of my friends who read the manuscript at different stages. Ellen Cohen, Larry Green, and Evan Sarzin offered many excellent suggestions. The editorial assistance of Melanie Fleishman and Amy Maddox of The Blue Pencil was invaluable.

I also appreciate the encouragement and advice I received from Ben Yagoda, Charlie Spicer, Dave Blinder, Vicki Polon, and Dr. Caroline Burmon, otherwise known as daughter number one.

Special thanks to daughter number two, thirteen-year-old Julia, for helping Dad avoid embarrassing himself completely when trying to capture how young teens speak these days. Although I do remain confused about a few things. You told me your friends never use the term "rock" to describe music. So what, I innocently asked, do you call Bruce Springsteen? "Old," you said. Sweetie, that is not helpful.

Thanks to my fantastic wife Adele Karig for being the book's first reader, for all of her editorial advice (she was an English major before becoming a tax lawyer), and for watching over Julia and our home when I hid myself away in my room. I think I'm almost ready to come out now.

Author Contact Page

If you enjoyed this book, I'd love to have your email address to let you know about new projects. You can reach me at andy@missinglincoln.com.

Watch for blog posts at www.missinglincoln.com and follow me on Facebook (andrew.feinberg.77) and Twitter (@afeinberg7).

About the Author

Andrew Feinberg is the author or co-author of five non-fiction books. An award-winning freelance writer, he has written for the *New York Times*, the *New York Times Magazine*, *GQ*, and *Barron's*. He has contributed more than 100 humor pieces to the *New York Times*, *Playboy*, and the *Wall Street Journal*, among other publications.

His sense of humor was severely challenged during several years as a corporate communications writer. When three of his clients—Dennis Kozlowski, Jeffrey Skilling, and Martha Stewart—were sent to prison, he took that as a sign to abandon the field. He spent fifteen years as a money manager—beating the S&P 500 over that period—and more than twenty years as a financial columnist for *Individual Investor* and *Kiplinger's Personal Finance*.

He received a B.A. in English from the University of Pennsylvania and an M.A. in Journalism from Stanford University. He and his family live in New York City. *Four Score and Seven* is his first novel.

He has been active in political campaigns since 1972, but nothing quite prepared him for the mayhem of the 2016 presidential campaign.

Made in the USA
San Bernardino, CA
13 April 2016